Copyright ©

CW00417363

All r

The characters and events por̶t̶r̶a̶y̶e̶d̶ ̶a̶r̶e̶
fictitious. Any similarity to real persons, living or dead, is
coincidental and not intended by the author.

No part of this book may be reproduced, or stored
in a retrieval system, or transmitted in any
form or by any means, electronic, mechanical,
photocopying, recording, or otherwise, without
express written permission of the publisher.

DEATH IN

RETREAT

A Bishop Farthing/Ken Jones story
By Paul Cosway

The Kingston Press

The talented thriller writer P D James asserted in her detective novel 'The Murder Room' that the motives for murder are always one of the four 'Ls': Love, Lust, Lucre or Loathing.

Well, She Is A Lucky Lady If She Never Felt The Evil, Crushing Grip Of Jealousy...

It begins...

The little boy curls up behind his bedroom door, struggling to stifle his sobs, to keep his grief secret – terrified his dad would hear and turn his anger on him. The colourful patterns on his wallpaper become grey and threatening, pressing in upon him, moving, swirling... From downstairs come screams and thuds. Each blow seems to thunder against his young chest, stopping his heart and leaving him battling to breathe.

His father's voice rasps through the closed door; tearing into the boy's mother: swearing, cursing. The child lives in dread of these nights - when his father becomes a monster and his mother, the next morning, is red eyed and bruised.

Eventually, after an eternity of suffering, the violence ends. His father drifts into a drunken stupor on the sofa downstairs and his mother crawls upstairs to bed. Then, tentatively, Kenny leaves his own room, creeps into his mother's bed, and snuggles up against her. In his own childish way, without saying a word, he's telling her I love you mum. I'll never hurt you. And when I grow up, I'll be strong. I'll protect you. And everyone like you.

Detective Inspector Ken Jones wakes with his fists tight, knuckles white, teeth clenched. The nightmare has become less frequent of late, but no less ugly. It always wakes him and leaves him reaching for his mother, but she is never there. He wipes the sweat from his brow and rolls over to look at the clock. Five fifteen. It is still dark outside. He groans and pulls the duvet over. It is hard to go back to sleep after these dreams – too many memories, too much hurt. But he will try. Two more hours if he can manage to drift off again. And the dreams never come twice on the same night. He promises himself he'll ring his mother if he gets a chance that afternoon. If the day is quiet enough to allow him the time. The care home allows calls between three and five – before the residents are led to supper and then bed. Not that his mother will understand – not even recognise his voice, probably. Week after week of blows to the head many years ago brought an early onset of Alzheimer's.

He was just falling back to sleep when the phone rang. His eyes didn't open. He groped a hand over to the bedside table and fumbled with the mobile. The ringing stopped before he could stab it with his finger. He dropped it on the carpet. 'If it's urgent, they'll ring again.'

DS Jenny Grace had a quick shower to wake herself up. As she dried her body with the bath sheet, she glanced critically into the mirror. For the past three months she had been on a strict diet. No carbohydrates, no sugars, no alcohol. Getting back into uniform for the funeral she'd attended with Ken, her boss, had been an unpleasant shock. She'd felt, well, dumpy. But, at last, the efforts she'd made had borne fruit. Her tummy looked flatter, her bum smaller. She'd gone down two dress sizes. She smiled at her reflection. Her beautiful, glossy brown skin seemed to smile back at her. Not perfect yet. Still too much on the hips. But she was beginning to feel good about herself. Even if no-one else seemed to notice.

She wrapped the towel around herself and rang Ken again. He rolled over in bed, groaning. He saw that the call was coming from his sergeant, Jenny, so he reached down and pressed 'Accept'.

'Hi Jen – what's up?'

'Sorry to wake you, boss.'

'What time is it?'

'Nearly six. We're needed.'

'More sheep gone missing?'

Jenny laughed. 'No, boss. A body,'

Ken was immediately wide awake. 'Where?'

'In the grounds of a Christian Retreat, just outside Marnhull. I'll send you the post code.'

'Oh great. A bunch of Jesus freaks!'

Jenny knew him well enough to realise he was joking.

'Good God-fearing people, boss, who I'm sure will do all they can to help the police with their enquiries.'

'I believe you. Thousands wouldn't. Okay, Jen. I'll call out a SOC team. It'll take at least an hour for them to get there. We'd better arrive first.'

'Roger, boss. I'll get dressed and set off straight away.'

'Are you hinting that you're talking to me naked?'

'Oh – I couldn't possibly say!'

'Best not! I'll be out in a couple of minutes. Meet you at the crime scene.'

'Okay, boss. See you there.'

Jenny dressed quickly. She was amused, but also slightly disturbed. Her boss, DI Ken Jones, had actually seen her naked once. The night they'd had sex after a party. Neither of them had talked of it since. She had resigned herself to the view that it had been a one night stand – nothing serious. But it hadn't felt like that at the time. She didn't entirely like that he was now joking about it. But she pushed this thought to the back of her mind and reached for her car keys.

Ken threw some water over his face. No time to shower. He dressed quickly in dark jeans and a plain blue short-sleeved shirt. He grabbed a navy hoody in case the weather was inclement and strode out to the small parking area where the residents of the close left their cars overnight. The houses were all one or two bedroomed starter homes in short terraces. The residents weren't wealthy. Their mortgages took most of their income. The other cars were generally old models in varying conditions, from fairly smart to dented and shabby. DI Jones' was the exception and the envy of his neighbours. His, leased from the force, was a new BMW with a dark, steely silvered finish that looked sleek and powerful. The blue lights were concealed behind the front grill.

Jenny just beat him to the entrance to the long drive that led to the Retreat and Ken followed her car up to the front door. The house was a large Georgian structure, its rendered front marked out with imitation courses of stone. In the early morning light, it looked in need of a good coat of paint. What was left was peeling and faded by many years of neglect. A stable and coach house block to the right had been adapted to provide additional accommodation. It reminded Ken of a care home or small private school that had fallen on very hard times. He pulled up beside the only other vehicle in sight – a police patrol car.

The traffic officer, sheltering in the doorway, looked mightily relieved to see reinforcements arrive.

'Good morning, sir. Good to see you.'

'Morning. There's a body?'

'Yes sir. I'll lead you there.'

'It's not in the house?'

'No sir. It's this way.'

The officer stepped smartly away from the house into the grounds. Ken waved to Jenny to follow them. For the first time, he took in the broader picture. They had parked on a wide shingle drive that led up to the main house. The lawns each side were overgrown. Beyond was woodland, a mixture of trees of varying types and ages. Everything reflected neglect. Those who lived here had other matters on their minds than general maintenance.

They picked their way through the undergrowth to a clearing by a small pond. Rushes and flag iris had taken it over and the few water lilies were struggling to survive. The water was dark and murky. Insects buzzed over it, a single damsel fly providing the only bright flash of colour as it passed through a beam of watery sunlight. There was a body lying at the water's edge, covered in a blanket.

'I thought it best to cover her, sir. I haven't touched anything.'

'Who found her?'

'One of the residents, sir. I have her name. I haven't managed to do any questioning – thought it better to stand guard until you arrived. The pathologist should be here any minute.'

Jenny looked up sharply. 'Who's coming?'

The officer looked surprised by the question. 'Er… A Doctor Peterson, I think.'

Jenny shot a wicked smirk in Ken's direction. 'Ah. Your girlfriend!'

Ken grunted and knelt down by the body. He eased the blanket down over the face. Grey eyes stared up at him, unseeing. The woman's hair was long, dark blonde and resting over part of her face, covering her mouth. She looked at peace, lying on her back. But as he pulled the blanket down further, he saw a gash across her neck. It had been cut. And then the reason for the blanket became clear. She was naked.

The silence was broken by the roar of several cars stirring up the gravel on the drive. The scene of crime team had arrived. Ken touched Jenny's arm. 'Stay here and watch over the site. I'll go and brief the team.'

Jenny smirked at him, 'Give her my love, won't you!' Ken didn't respond to this private joke between them, apart from giving her a rueful smile in return. He strode quickly back to the house. He was tall, just over six feet, and moved with the ease of an athlete. He ran a hand through his thick brown hair as he prepared to face the newcomers. Organising the SOC team would be straightforward. That was routine. But if Sheila Peterson had arrived already – how to respond to her presence was much more of a problem. They had history. And how.

The members of the SOC team were clambering into their plastic over-suits. Ken identified Jock, the Scotsman who had worked with him on many other investigations. He was, outwardly, a dour man with a shock of hair, a red beard, and a Shetland pullover no matter what the weather. But Ken knew that he had a good sense of humour and that he took his job very seriously indeed. If there were clues to be found, Jock and his team would uncover them. The ruddy face creased into a cynical smile as Ken approached him.

'Och, dunna tell me they've put a wee babe in charge!'

Ken joshed back. 'Aye, grandad. It's lucky you're here to hold my hand!'

'I'm no holding your hand, you ken. If you want to come out, you can choose some other fairy to do it wi'!'

They shook hands warmly and Ken ensured that Jock knew the lie of the land – where the body was situated and the initial area of interest. Jock was organising the fixing of the boundary of blue and white police tape, to keep intruders out, as Ken finally looked round to ascertain if the pathologist had arrived. She had. Her car was parked a few metres away and Sheila was still sitting in her car, putting her elegant feet into the overshoes that looked from a distance like large plastic carrier bags. He didn't walk towards her as he once would. He waited until she had finished and got to her feet.

'Follow that path.' He realised that he was being discourteous. It was not his normal way. He was always polite, even to crooks. But Sheila had treated him badly and there was still anger deep inside him. He hadn't even greeted her. She stared at him in surprise, as he continued, 'She's down the slope. Next to a small pond. Jenny's waiting for you.'

'You're not coming with me? To show me the way?' Her eyes were flecked with green. He'd never noticed that before. She had applied eye shadow carefully to complement the colour. She stood her ground coolly, her gaze steady.

'I'll join you later. I've got to instruct the SOC team.'

Sheila didn't move. 'I'd rather you were with me. I'll wait.'

Involuntarily, his fists clenched. For a moment he was back in her apartment, that evening six months ago. They'd looked out together at the view from her windows – the sun setting over a sparkling sea. She'd cooked them a meal. Offered him a glass of red wine. He had sipped it, wondering if she'd suggest another. She didn't. It wasn't intended then that he should stay the night. Then came the long, rambling explanation of her predicament. She liked him. Maybe he was the one for her. But she was in a relationship. It would have to end before they could be together. She wasn't prepared to two-time anyone, and she didn't think he would agree to that either. So, he would have to wait, whilst she disentangled herself. Like it or leave it.

It got worse. The other man was her boss – more than twenty years her senior (Old enough, he thought bitterly, to be her dad) and much older than Ken. So, this was her ultimatum. Hang around, kick your heels, while I still sleep with someone else until I'm ready to dump him and give you your turn. He'd realised over time how manipulative she was. How much she expected to get her own way. A very beautiful woman who'd been used to having men fawning over her – always doing her bidding. Had she finally freed herself? Was he now in the running? Well, think on, Sheila. I'm not your toy to pick up when it suits you and drop when it doesn't.

Wordlessly he turned and began to walk towards where the body was lying, cold and still, beneath her modesty blanket. He glanced round to see if Sheila was following. She was, a few feet behind, with an amused smile on her face. He passed the corpse and stood beside Detective Sergeant Jenny Grace, as if to make it clear that he was closer to his assistant than to this woman he had once loved.

Doctor Sheila Peterson pulled a small recorder from her bag and scanned the area to find a spot that was least likely to dirty her knees. Then she knelt beside the body. She pulled back the covering. 'The victim is a young woman, between twenty and thirty in age. No sign of bruising to the face, but damage to her hair.' She lifted the head slightly, her fingers cupping under the skull and raising it gently. 'It has been pulled back and clumps of hair have been torn from the scalp, presumably to jerk her head back hard. The neck has been sliced part way through with a sharp blade. There's significant loss of blood. Initial finding is that this cut would have been the cause of death. The blood has run down between her breasts, so she must have been upright when the throat was lacerated.'

Sheila moved so that she was between the body and the police officers before pulling the blanket down to the woman's knees. 'There's no sign of sexual trauma. No bruising to indicate any sexual violence, but I'll need to examine the body back at the mortuary in more detail to be sure.' With that she pulled the blanket back over the victim's face. 'Has the photographer arrived?'

Ken nodded. 'He's with the SOC team.'

'He can take the pictures now. Then put her in a body bag and send her down to me.'

'Of course.'

The pathologist was still a moment, looking squarely at Ken. There was clearly more that she wanted to say, but, with Jenny there, she decided the time was not right. 'I'll let you know when I'm ready to conduct the post-mortem. You can call round and we'll discuss the findings?'

Ken shrugged. 'Of course.'

Another moment of stillness. Then she decided to be mildly amused by his reticence. 'Okay then. It's a date.' And she turned and made her way slowly and carefully along the path to her car. She stepped round the brambles to ensure that she didn't snag her stockings.

Jenny squeezed Ken's arm. 'Well, that told her!' She was secretly pleased that Ken had put her down, though she didn't hold out hope that he would ever look upon her the way he had Sheila. Ken smiled ruefully. 'Come on. We'd better get to work.'

Together they walked back to the front of the building where the solitary constable still kept guard. He looked impatient to be back in his patrol car, working to keep the roads safe. 'I'm afraid you'll have to hang around here a while longer,' Ken told him. 'I'll get someone to relieve you as soon as I can.'

'Understood, sir. Not a problem, sir.'

'Are the people inside ready for questioning? We'd better start with whoever's in charge.'

The officer looked uncertain. 'Err – that might be difficult, sir.'

'Difficult? Why?'

A shuffle of the feet and a long intake of breath. 'They're not... They said not to disturb them, sir.'

Ken's eyebrows lifted in surprise. 'I'd have thought they'd be eager to help; to find the culprit! After all – she was one of their own, wasn't she?'

'Yes sir. But – well – they're busy, sir!'

'Well, they can bloody unbusy themselves! There's a body over there!'

'They're busy...praying sir!'

He stood aside smartly as Ken and Jenny pushed past him and strode into the house. A large entrance hall. The little light there was came through the front door. There were no windows. At first, they struggled to see anything. Ahead of them a wide staircase materialised out of the gloom and led their eyes up to the landing level. From a niche in the wall at the top, a plaster statue of a saint stared down at them, disapprovingly, painted tears on her cheeks.

Heavy wooden doors led to ground floor rooms, but there was no clue as to what lay beyond them. The overwhelming impression was that everything was dark and brown. Turning back to the entrance door, they could now make out a heavy wooden crucifix hanging over it, looking likely to drop at any moment onto the unsuspecting head of any trespasser.

Jenny shuddered. 'Gloomy hole! Gives me the collywobbles!'

Ken nodded. 'It's hardly full of Christian joy and light!' He raised a hand. 'Listen!'

They froze for a moment and then made out the sound of voices. Ken walked from door to door to locate the origin of the sound. He stopped to the left of the staircase at a huge mahogany door, with heavy panelling. He put his ear to it.

He heard a man's voice intoning: 'Eternal rest grant unto her, Oh Lord, and may perpetual light shine upon her.' There was a chorus of amen from what sounded like a large group of females. 'May our late beloved sister rest in eternal peace, in Your love always.' Again, a chorus of amen.

Ken looked at Jenny. She shrugged. 'We'd better push in.' She nodded and he turned the brass handle. The hinges had not been oiled for many years. As the door swung open, their arrival was broadcast to the room's occupants by a very loud and very ugly screech. Heads turned. The room's curtains, of a thick dark velvet, were closed so that almost no light drifted in to illuminate the faces of those gathered within. On a dais at the far end, behind a lectern with a brass eagle, a man stood. His wild hair and unkempt beard reminiscent of an Old Testament prophet. Before him, seated on benches, were about twenty five women and children. He saw the two interlopers and scowled.

With a wave of his hand, he dismissed them, indicating that they should return the way they had come. His gesture was the same he would use to swat at an annoying fly. Ken ignored him and continued to advance, while Jenny hovered by the door. Conscious of her religious upbringing, she wondered if the man was in fact a priest. She was afraid of causing offence. When the leader of the small congregation realised that Ken was not following his instruction, the prophet look-a-like pointed at a woman on the back row, pointed to Ken, and waved to her to deal with him.

She rose obediently but looked dazed. She signalled to Ken to follow her and tiptoed to the door. Ken sized up the dais man. No more than five seven. He looked taller, raised up on the lectern. But with his feet on the ground, Ken would tower over him. He smiled to himself. For the moment, he would do as he was bid. But a reckoning would come.

But, for now, the prayers resumed: 'Almighty and eternal God, from whose love in Christ we cannot be parted, either in death or life, hear our prayers and thanksgivings for her whom we remember this day, fulfil in her the purpose of your love, and bring us all with her to your eternal joy...'

He joined Jenny in the hallway. The woman who'd

been allocated to deal with them stood, head bowed, next to the grand staircase. She wore no make-up. Her hair, light brown, was tied back severely from her face. Very pale, with large brown eyes, she reminded Ken of a timid – and scared – hamster. Like the others, she wore an A line dress of plain white fabric that reached almost to her feet. The three-quarter sleeves, slightly baggy, made her arms and hands look pathetically thin. She looked up as they approached. 'It's my duty day. If anyone calls – from the outside – I 'ave to deal with it.'

Jenny jumped in. 'Is he your leader? The man leading your prayers?'

'Bless his heart. He's our link with the Almighty. He's guardian of our souls.'

Ken wondered if she was on something. He attempted to bring the discussion down to earth. 'You're praying for her? The dead woman in the wood?'

She opened her eyes wide, startled by his brusqueness.

'Our sister in Heaven!'

Ken's eyes widened. 'She was your sister?'

Jenny interjected, 'Are they all your sisters? All the women in there?' She indicated the room they had vacated. The woman nodded. 'Yeah. We're all sisters in the eyes of Christ.'

Ken rolled his eyes. He wondered if she could say anything original, or would just repeat what she'd been told, like a well-trained politician. He'd keep trying. He needed to establish some facts. 'I'm Detective Inspector Jones. This is my assistant, Detective Sergeant Grace. And you are?'

She lifted her head and looked him full in the face, her eyes wide and wondering. 'I'm sister Luke.' She smiled, as if childishly proud of herself. 'Like the apostle, innit.'

'Thank you, sister.' Jenny frowned, eager to help Ken. 'Your name before you became a sister. That's the one we need. Who were you then?'

The woman's eyes glazed over, as if she was searching deep into her memory, for a time long lost. 'It wa' Jen.' More concentration. 'Marshall, weren'tit. Jen Marshall.'

Jenny wrote this down. 'Thank you, Jen. And the lady in the wood. Her name?'

'Sister Charity.'

'No – her real name. Before she joined you.'

The woman shook her head, her mouth hanging slightly open. Ken was losing patience. Was this an act, or was she really this dopey? 'Surely you know?' She shook her head again. 'We need to talk to the man leading you. We need access to your records. There must be a filing system. There must be some record of who you all are! We need to get him out of there!'

But as he turned back to the door, Sister Luke grabbed his sleeve. 'No! It's forbidden, innit!' She was highly agitated. 'While the Leader's…doin' his prayers…no-one can…you mustn't!'

Jenny intervened. 'Better give them a few more minutes, boss. We should show respect for their beliefs.'

Ken turned back to Sister Luke. 'A few more minutes. How long is it likely to last?'

The woman shrugged. 'Dunno. Hours.'

Ken broke away from her. He opened the door and stared in. Then he turned back to Sister Luke. 'Is there a – sort of – boss sister?'

Jenny tried to help. She spoke gently to their confused informant. 'Is there a second in command to the man – leader – who can answer our questions?' Sister Luke gave her a worried glance then pointed, reluctantly, to a woman with long blonde hair, standing head bowed at the end of the last row of the seats. Ken walked determinedly over to her and touched her arm. When she turned, he gestured to her to follow him to the hallway. She turned to check with the leader. He had his back to them, praying silently for the moment, staring up at the shaft of sunlight from a window high above him. Lacking guidance from him, she slowly, and reluctantly, did as she was bid.

'Who is she?' Jenny asked.

Sister Luke did a splendid impersonation of a frightened rabbit. 'Mercy!'

'Pardon?'

'Sister Mercy,' she repeated.

Mercy's eyes, as she assessed her questioners, were bright and alert. Ken deduced that she could prove more informative than her friend. But she was equally in thrall to the bearded man who was fronting the service. When asked how long it might last, she smiled proudly. 'We cannot tell. Once the leader is touched by the Holy Spirit his inspiration is without bounds! He once led us in prayer for almost twelve hours without pause for rest or refreshment!'

Taller and slimmer than Sister Luke, her white cotton dress seemed to fit better. Almost elegant. The little of her legs that could be viewed revealed that they were shapely with trim ankles. Like Luke she wore sliders on her feet, but her toenails were painted rather than raw. She looked at Ken questioningly: an attractive face devoid of make-up, her eyebrows raised slightly.

Ken got down to business. 'Is there somewhere we can sit and talk?'

Sister Mercy looked uncomfortable. 'I don't know. I should join the service…'

'Just a little while,' Jenny coaxed. 'We understand

your need to pray for your lost friend, but you may be able to help: to help find her killer. The sooner we can begin the better. Surely they can spare you?'

Sister Mercy was not convinced but, as Luke crept silently back into the meeting room, she reluctantly led them to the opposite side of the hall and opened a door that led into a drawing room with an assortment of shabby but comfortable chairs. Dark religious paintings lined the walls. A framed text read, 'Be sure: your sin will find you out!' Ken walked up to it. 'Cheerful!'

'It's from the Old Testament, boss.' Jenny's childhood visits with her mother to church stood her in good stead. 'Numbers, I think.' Ken looked confused. 'It's a book in the Bible. Numbers.'

He accepted this with a shrug and indicated a chair to Mercy. As she sat, he took a chair facing her and began. 'We need all the help you can give us. This is a murder enquiry. Even trivial details could help us with our investigation.'

Jenny noticed that the woman was not sitting comfortably. Rather, she perched on the edge of the chair, nervously, as if desperate for escape. Jenny sought to reassure her, 'We won't take long, love. But this is important. We have to do our job. Do you understand?' She nodded but didn't relax. Jenny opened her notebook discreetly so as not to alarm her any more than necessary.

Ken gave Jenny an appreciative glance, aware that

she was trying to help, and began. 'Did the victim – Sister...'

'Charity,' Jenny interjected.

'Thanks. Sister Charity – did she have any enemies? Did anyone have a grudge against her?'

'Here?'

'Yes, in your community.'

The woman looked shocked. 'We live here in love and peace!'

Jenny reached over to touch the woman's arm reassuringly. When she reacted like a frightened rabbit, Jenny drew back but continued with another question. 'In a closed community like this, even one built on love, there must sometimes be tensions?'

She stared back as if not understanding, or not realising that it was a question to which she was supposed to respond. Ken realised that mercy did not seem to strain to giving information freely. He decided to concentrate on practicalities. 'We're looking for a knife. Where would knives be kept? In the kitchen?' She nodded, dumbly. 'Can you take me there?'

As she rose to comply, Jenny tried another approach. 'I need the ladies. Is it upstairs?'

'Yes. On the left. Second door.'

The kitchen was fairly clean. And almost tidy.

There was a wide assortment of cups draining by the sink. He looked round for a knife rack. If one was missing, it would point to a possible suspect in the community. But it wasn't that sort of kitchen. Rather than a carefully planned selection of cutlery and cooking utensils, it seemed that objects had just been gathered at random over many years. 'Knives?' Sister Luke pointed to a drawer. It was full of knives. Some short, some long, some sharp and many blunt. No sign of blood. And no way of knowing if one was missing.

Jenny reached the top of the stairs and opened the first door she came to. It was a large bedroom, around twenty feet square. Two bunk beds for children and three single beds with a bedside cabinet by each. Clothes were hung on rails or stacked neatly on the floor. The occupants certainly live frugally, she thought. She wondered if one of the beds had belonged to the woman lying dead outside. A quick look round, and then a swift rifle through the contents of the cabinets, to search for clues at least to the true identities of the occupants. She was lucky. The occasional passport, driving licence or credit card – she rapidly inserted names and addresses into her notebook.

Putting everything back to rights as well as she could – without a warrant she was on dangerous ground – she left the room and opened the next door. A similar dormitory. The same rapid search for names.

Ken abandoned the drawers in the kitchen and tried again to eke information from Sister Mercy. 'The woman we found – Sister Charity – she's been murdered! Do you understand?' The woman nodded. Ken was struggling. He expected a stronger response – tears, distress – at the loss of a close companion. 'We want to find her killer and need your help – the help of everyone who lives here!' Again a nod, but not a word, not a blink, not a tear. Ken tried another line of questioning. 'When we found her, she was naked. Out there – many yards from the house. By the pond. Wearing nothing. Does that seem strange to you? Would you expect one of your group to be outside, naked?'

Mercy stared at him with wide eyes that expressed surprise that he would even ask such a question. Ken prompted again, 'You think it's normal?'

At last, she spoke. 'The Leader tells us that God gave us our bodies. Were not Adam and Eve meant to live without clothing in the Garden of Eden? Was it not because of their sin that they covered their bodies? How can there be anything shameful about the flesh that God gave us to wrap around our immortal souls?'

Ken wasn't sure that the story of Eden was much more than a myth, but this wasn't the time for a theological argument. 'So he tells you to walk around outside…stark naked?'

She nodded, as if this was the most natural thing in the world. Which perhaps it is.

'All of you?' Again a nod. 'Every day?'

'For some part of the day. When He blesses us with weather that is kind. It's our way of showing God how grateful we are for the bodies He has given us. We are the most wonderful of His creations, are we not?' And she held up her arms to the heavens. Or at least to the kitchen ceiling. As she did so, her cotton dress pulled tight across her body. With a choking feeling, Ken suddenly realised that she was naked under the thin cotton. He felt a slight moment of panic. He wanted Jenny back.

But his second in command was opening yet another door. And this room was different. It contained just one bed – a large king size with white covers, spread with pillows and cushions in rich shades of purple and mauve. It was a four-poster with elaborate hangings. She speculated that this must be the bedroom of the man they called their leader. There were mirrors on the walls, alternating with pictures that were disturbingly erotic. Much about this felt wrong to Jenny. She used the camera on her phone to record the details and swiftly left. The room was well kept but felt somehow sordid. Everything about it made Jenny feel uncomfortable. She had stayed upstairs as long as she dared. Unwilling to arouse suspicion, she closed the door quietly and crept silently down the stairs to re-join her boss.

He was still trying to get information from the only member of the community available to them. 'Is there an office? Somewhere where records are kept? The names and addresses of all the people here?' Sister Mercy gave a look that expressed a total lack of understanding and slowly shook her head, as if he'd been asking her for the whereabouts of the Holy Grail.

But Jenny had seen the dormitories and knew that some information was available from there. 'Could you show us,' she asked gently, 'where Sister Charity slept? Her bedroom?"

Ken looked at her in surprise, very conscious they were on thin ice, exploring the building without a warrant. Jenny winked at him to provide some reassurance. But Sister Mercy looked troubled. 'You mean when she isn't…?'

It was Ken's turn to be confused, but Jenny's mind was on overdrive. She had a clear idea of what the woman meant. 'Yes. Her own bed. When she was on her own.'

Sister Mercy stared at the closed door, behind which the service of remembrance still continued, as if seeking permission. Then, obviously uncertain, she walked slowly to the staircase. 'Here. Up here.'

Ken guessed she was in her thirties, but she was

walking up very hesitantly. He began to wonder if there were drugs involved. Were these women high on something? However, Jenny followed the sister confidently. And she wasn't surprised when, as they reached the landing that she had already explored, Mercy continued to where a further stair led up to the third floor. Here were the attic rooms, with sloping ceilings, heavy wooden beams and narrow dormer windows. She opened the furthest door. It led into a small, whitewashed room with a single bed, a crucifix on the wall, a small desk with a prayer cushion in front and a small cupboard with a broken door. In this, Jenny could see papers that might give them the information they needed.

But first, she wanted to check out the other occupants of this upper floor. 'Is your room up here?' Sister Mercy shook her head. 'So these are for?'

'The leader has…special ones. Sisters who are his comforters. I have not yet risen.'

'These are ones, perhaps, without children, but who sometimes sleep downstairs – but not alone?' Sister Mercy nodded, her eyes tearful. There was a ranking here that was causing her some distress. Ken was struggling to keep up with this. Jenny pressed on. 'There could be papers here that would tell us her name and her home address. I need to look in this cupboard!'

Sister Mercy stepped back in dismay. It went against her instincts to go through someone's private things, but she couldn't think of any way to stop Jenny as she bent down and passed documents to her boss.

Ken was appreciative. 'That's great, Jen. Here's the name: Jean Metcalf. And letters and a driving licence – all with her home address. At least we can contact the next of kin and get the body officially identified.'

Sister Mercy looked unhappy and Jenny was quick to put her at ease. 'You've been really helpful, love. You've done nothing wrong. We'll go back down, shall we? See if the service is over?' She nodded and followed them, but Jenny's optimism was misplaced. As they neared the door of the conference room, they could hear the intoning of prayers and then the congregation burst into song – some kind of spiritual.

Ken realised that Jenny was on to something and needed a chance to talk to him alone. He told Mercy they didn't need her help anymore. They were going to leave. She could re-join the service. And she seemed mightily relieved to do just that.

Ken checked with the SOC team leader on progress as soon as he got outside. There was little to report. They had not found any evidence of the murder weapon yet. Jenny waited in his car, where they could talk without being overheard. As soon as he joined her, she voiced her concerns.

'There's a lot that's fishy about this, boss. One – this whole retreat thing. The whole idea of a retreat is somewhere to spend a couple of days in sort of quiet contemplation and prayer – to find yourself. I've come across them before. Not gone to one, but I know how they work. This one is a joke. These women seem to be living here permanently. Who pays for it? Have they no jobs? No partners? And two: this leader. He seems to have them in thrall. He has some sort of power over them. And there are two levels, do you see? Middle floor dormitories for the ones with children – or the plainer, dopey ones like our friend Sister Luke. And single rooms upstairs for - what did she call them? The chosen ones. Those are the ones he's shagging!'

'You're sure?'

'Look boss!' And she turned on her phone and scrolled through the pictures she'd taken of his bedroom.

'Bloody hell! Who's responsible for this setup? This retreat? It's a church thing, isn't it?'

'The ones I've heard of through our church are run by the diocese. But I don't know. It could be some sort of charity. Or a donation from some wealthy well wisher who hopes it will get him into Heaven and his sins forgiven!'

'I thought that sort of thing had died out with the destruction of the monasteries. Let's check it out.' He called the office. 'Who's that? Geoff? We've got some info on the victim.' He gave him the name and address and asked him to find the next of kin. Also: 'Can you contact the office of the bishop and ask them about the Christian Retreat at Marnhull. Yes – where the body's been found. See if it belongs to them, will you? If it does, we need to check out who's using it and how.'

'Will do, boss. Oh and Doctor Peterson's been trying to contact you.'

Jenny gave a coy smile. 'Oh, she has, has she? Well…maybe I should get out of the car and leave you together!'

'Don't be daft!' He found her mobile number 'Hello Sheila. I understand you've been trying to call. I had to turn off the phone while we were in the building. What've you got?'

'Well. Hello Ken. I've been waiting here for you. I was hoping you'd call by.' Jenny giggled and Ken gave her a stern stare. 'I've got some preliminary findings for you. Want to come over?'

Ken sighed. He knew that he was still strongly attracted to Sheila, though he believed she'd treated him badly and could be cold and calculating. But at that moment, there was no question of leaving the scene of the crime. 'We've still got lots to do here, Sheila. I'll call you as soon as I'm free.'

She didn't seem too put out by this possible put-down. 'That's fine, Ken. I'll be at my apartment this evening. Call by.'

Another giggle from Jenny. Ken pursed his lips. Not, maybe, such a good outcome. Still there was work to do. He put the pathologist out of his mind and concentrated on the task in hand. 'What do we do, Jen? We need to question everyone here. How long is this service going to last?'

'No idea. But it's a prayer meeting, boss. We can't just barge in and drag people out.' She looked thoughtful. 'Seems to me it's more a cult than a retreat. But not a cult with a special doctrine or purpose. More of a harem...'

As the two detectives stared glumly at the building that might hold the secrets to the crime they were investigating, it seemed to stare back at them inscrutably, tall trees casting dark shadows across the stuccoed front.

Fifteen miles away, the quiet Dorset village of Bishop Farthing was bathed in sunshine. Its occupants had varied backgrounds. Some were newcomers enjoying the calm and peace of North Dorset, having escaped there from the frenzy of city living. Others, born and bred in the hamlets around, hardly knew a life beyond. All faced one of the important decisions of the day – what to have for lunch.

In an attractive terraced cottage, one of the newcomers, Margot, smiled at her baby, propped up quietly in her playpen. She thought for the thousandth time how lucky she was with Summer. Such a placid child, hardly ever any trouble. She was sleeping through the night now. Unwilling to be parted from her for even a night, she slept in the bed with the child and Margot would coo softly when the baby stirred. This seemed to calm her and her little eyes would soon close again. She had never loved anything so much in all her long life – for this was a late baby. And she had never felt so much devotion in return. Margot was a single mum and that's how she wanted it. Just the two of them.

She had a regular routine. She had read in the Mother and Baby magazine that children respond best to a strict timetable. Meals always at the same time each day. Naps morning and afternoon. Bed at a set time. Don't feed them when they think they're hungry. If you do, they'll begin to demand milk whenever they want attention. It may seem cruel sometimes, but it's best in the long run, for both mother and baby, to stick to a timetable.

Half eleven. Time for some fresh air. Margot picked her munchkin gently from the pen and wrapped her in a soft blanket. She stroked her cheek tenderly as her pride and joy seemed to give her a tiny smile. A kiss on the forehead and then she went out the front and tucked baby into her carrycot in the garden. She smiled. Summer had come and filled her life with sunshine. Margot went back inside to compose her lunchtime sandwich. She thought her heart would burst with happiness.

Back at the retreat, however, Ken was far from happy. 'Sorry Jenny. We can't just sit here and do nothing. Can you check back with Geoff and see what he's got so far on the victim? What's her name?'

'Jean Metcalf, boss. The address on her driving licence was in Winterborne Kingston.'

'We'll need a next of kin at least. Ask Geoff and Ange to check out the house, see if there's any family. They need to know what's happened and tell us if there was anyone who could have harmed her. Meantime, I'm going to get the top man out of that prayer meeting.'

'Wow, boss! This'll be a first! A memorial service is sort of sacrosanct!'

'That's why I'll go in alone. Keep you out of it. There's no choice. You heard what Sister Luke said. This could go on all day and all night!'

'Good luck, boss. You know I'd go in with you.' Her loyalty was never in doubt.

'Thanks, but no need.' He left the car and

strolled determinedly towards the entrance. Jenny watched him. He walked like an athlete, fit and strong. Some officers got flabby and drank too much. But for Ken physical fitness was an important attribute for his job. She watched him as he took the steps two at a time. Her thoughts were not all on the task in hand.

But her attention was drawn almost immediately to an elderly lady who had walked unsteadily to the blue and white tape and was trying to duck beneath it. Jenny left the car and walked over. 'I'm sorry, dear. This is a crime scene. You can't come in.'

'They need me in there. You'll have to help me under, duck.'

'They need you? You'll have to tell me why.'

'They can't do nothing for themselves. It'll be a right bloody mess if I don't get in to clean up after them!'

Jenny lifted the tape, helped her through and guided her to the car. 'Sit in here for a minute. I'd like to ask you a few questions.'

'Well, you'll have to be quick. I've got to get back to cook dinner!'

Jenny ignored the woman's grumpy tone. 'What's your name, dear?'

As she took notes, Jenny looked carefully at the unexpected visitor. Her hair was a shock of white.

Even though it was a warm day, her clothing was intended for comfort rather than fashion. She wore an old, faded cardigan buttoned up to the top. A pair of thick woollen jogger bottoms that had been dark blue once but were now pale round the knees and bum and spattered with stains. The lower parts were obscured by chunky wool socks, one of which was badly holed. 'Do you live here?'

'No, I bloody don't. I'm the caretaker, ain't I?'

'But you're...you're too...'

'Old? Is that it? Course I am. Eighty-three years. But I've still got my wits about me, young woman!'

'I'm sure you have, ma'am. But you're the caretaker? They pay you?'

'I should be so lucky! I get nowt. I do it as a favour, don't I? For the church. Used to get a stipend, I did. But I got too old. They said I'd have to retire. I said not bloody likely. I've looked after this place most of my life. I'll not stop now. Money's short, they said. Got to cut back. Don't seem to have affected the bishop, mind, he still does all right!'

Jenny wisely ignored this. 'The group that's in there now – how long have they been here?'

'Bloody ages. Started to turn up last January. Then more came. Dribs and drabs. Six, seven months. It's not right. I told the office. It's a retreat, not a bloody holiday home. They don't care, as long as the rent's paid. It's got hard to get people to stay here. Over the past three or four years. Nobody wants retreats no more. They'd rather stay at home and watch telly!'

'Why's that? Why don't people want to come? Is there anything…dangerous?'

'Naw. Run down, ain't it? Folks want their comforts now. Don't want to share a bathroom with a dozen other people. Heating don't work half the time. Old mattresses. That lot - them in there - don't care. Daft as they come. And wandering round in the nuddy. I've seen 'em. Disgusting, I say.'

'And the man who's in charge?'

'I'm safe enough. Old and ugly, that's me. But you want to watch yourself, duck. He'll have his hand in your pants before you can say hallelujah and amen. I have to change the beds, duck. I could tell ya some tales that'll make your hair curl!'

Jenny accepted the warning without comment and pressed on. 'What are relationships like, inside the house? Do they all get on? Would any of them have any reason to - well – harm each other?'

'Oh aye. They fight like cats in there. They all want him.'

'The leader?'

'Aye. They're all fighting over 'im. God alone knows why. Like cats on heat. Chasing after a bloody beard. He's all front. Prophet he calls himself. It's profit he's after. I reckon he's taking them stupid bitches for all they've got!'

She turned to go but Jenny caught her arm. 'Taking them? You mean for money?'

The woman scowled. 'I know what the church charges. For rent. And a couple of the poor bints in there told me how much they're paying him to be part of his circus. Someone's raking it in. But what do I know? I'm just the caretaker. Unpaid. More fool me, huh?'

As the woman hobbled towards the front door, Jenny frowned. There was a lot here that was wrong. On impulse, she called Geoff back at base and asked him to check out the finances of the retreat. Then decided this was the time to join Ken inside. She doubted that the elderly caretaker had any hard evidence to back up her claims, but she could be questioned further later. The priority now was to acquaint Ken with what she'd been told.

In Bishop Farthing, Annette was sauntering past Margot's on her way home from the village shop. She was dressed for a warm and leisurely day. She'd tied her dark hair into a ponytail secured with a pink scrunchy she'd borrowed from her daughter. She'd dressed in a pale grey jogging suit but had no intention of breaking into a sweat. There was no need to hurry. She wanted to enjoy the warm sunshine, the buzzing of the insects, and the quiet country lanes.

And when she saw the pram outside Margot's front door, she decided to peep in. She liked babies. Once or twice before she'd been tempted to walk up and smile at the little bundle of joy, but hadn't dared. Margot was so protective of the child that she wrapped her in enough sheets and blankets to smother a less resilient baby. And as she had never invited Annette to hold the child, she had kept a respectful distance.

But Annette had a sudden unexpected rush of anxiety. And the closer she got, the more worried she became. Annette had the sight – or so her neighbours believed. In truth she did seem to have some sort of intuition. If she thought a child was ill, she was usually right. If she thought a pet would recover and didn't need expensive visits to the vet – it would generally recover without spending a fortune on fees. Her neighbours had come to trust her. They at least had confidence in her hunches. And as she approached the pram, her psychic alarm bells were tingling.

But when she reached it, there was no obvious reason for concern. There was no baby in distress. There was no baby at all. Annette thought that Margot must have taken her indoors. The covers had been neatly pulled down. There was just a depression in the bottom sheet where the child had been.

Annette ought to have moved on. But something held her there. Margot, she knew, was a creature of habit: everything in her life ran to a strict timetable. They'd had the occasional good-natured disagreement over the way that this impinged on childcare. Annette had always responded to her own baby's cries – providing a hug or an early feed if her children seemed to need one. Margot insisted the child fitted in with the mother's regime. If you give in too often, she asserted, the child will start to rule the home. Annette, in the end, had to agree, grudgingly, that it seemed to work – especially for Margot. Her child, Summer, was proving far less demanding than any of Annette's offspring. She seemed an ideal baby. Good as gold. Annette turned to continue her walk home. Then stopped.

Try as she might, she couldn't get the idea that something was wrong out of her head. She checked the time on her phone. Quarter to twelve. Day after day, Margot left the baby out in the fresh air until twelve. It gave her time to do a bit of housework, wash, dress, relax in front of the telly for an hour, and prepare lunch before bringing Summer indoors for her feed.

But it was quarter to twelve. And the pram was empty, even though the child was always left outside until midday.

Why had she taken her in early? Had she been crying? Certainly possible. But it would be unusual for Margot to respond to that. Was the baby ill?

Was Margot all right?

Annette turned and then stopped again. She was making a fuss about nothing. What would she say when Margot answered the door? I was worried because you took Summer in half an hour early? Because you're anal and always do everything at the same time, day after day? Because I've always gently mocked the way you run your life to a timetable and now I'm worried because you're not following it?

She turned away. Took a few steps. Paused again. She needed an excuse to call. It came to her. Sally Jones. The single girl with the lockdown baby. She was offering to babysit for her neighbours to earn a little money. Sally's mother had begun looking after her grandson to help Sally out while she earned a few pounds, looking after other people's children. Did Margot know? Annette didn't think she'd been out once since Summer arrived. That was when Margot too had become part of their village community.

And with Sally's help she could get out, make new friends. She could socialise. Go to the village film shows. Attend a meeting of the garden club. Annette convinced herself that it all made perfect sense. More confident now, she strode up to Margot's door and knocked.

Margot was happy to see her. Invited her in. And she seemed pleased to hear about Sally (although on reflection, she thought Summer was too young to be left yet). Annette wasn't surprised. She hadn't expected that Margot would take up the offer. It had just been an excuse to get inside the house. She looked round but couldn't see the baby. 'You brought her in early today! Was she crying?'

Margot looked totally confused. 'What?'

'I looked in the pram. She's not there... You brought her in? Didn't you?'

The blood drained from Margot's face. Her eyes widened with fear. 'My baby...where's my baby?'

Ken sent the traffic officer away. There was no longer a need to guard the entrance, so he could resume his normal duties, much to his relief. Standing around for so long had been a strain, especially on his bladder.

Back into the dark and cavernous hall. Ken stood beside the door to the meeting room and drew in breath as he listened. He heard the self-styled prophet intoning yet another prayer for the newly deceased. This was the most difficult entry he had ever made. Sure of his legal right to question whomsoever he wanted, he was less sure of his moral rights. Disturbing a religious service – even one without end – went against all his upbringing. It showed a lack of respect that went against the grain. But it had to be done. Putting his doubt and uncertainty on hold, he pushed against the door and entered, assuming an expression of confident authority.

Hardly any of the congregation took notice of him. Two of the children turned their faces in his direction. One pulled his thumb from his mouth in surprise. But the leader had his back to Ken, gazing up at the beam of sunshine that had burst in more bravely than the detective from a window high above. He addressed this stream of photons as he gave praise to the Lord for the gift of Sister Charity – even though she had been allowed to remain with them for such a tragically short time.

With more courage than he felt, Ken walked smartly to the front of the room and tapped the prophet on the shoulder. As prophets go, this one seemed to have difficulty foretelling the future, for this took him completely by surprise. Once he regained his composure, he attempted to put Ken in his place. 'Detective?'

'That's right, sir. Detective Inspector Kenneth Jones. I have a number of questions that I need to ask you. It's a matter of urgency. We need your help with our enquiries into the murder of a young woman who was a member of your group here.'

Unimpressed, the man waved his arm dismissively. 'As you can see, we are engaged in the Lord's work here. Earthly business will have to wait until that of Heaven is done!'

But two of the children took advantage of Ken's interruption to make a point of their own. They were thirsty. And tired. A mother whispered an apology and tried to smuggle them from the room without drawing attention to herself. But failed. Other children began to wail in support of their young brethren. They too were tired. And, it turned out, thirsty. And hungry. So yet another mother was lost to the service. Closely followed by two more. The prophet decided, reluctantly, to make the best of a bad situation. He announced a short break for refreshment and the room emptied with remarkable alacrity.

'Well, inspector, you seem to have succeeded in gaining my attention. I trust that the Lord will forgive you for this unwarranted intrusion upon our acts of devotion. Be not deceived, inspector; God is not mocked; for whatsoever a man soweth, so shall he reap! Galatians, chapter six, verse seven!'

Ken flicked open his notepad. 'Precisely so. And it is my job to ensure that whoever committed this crime suffers the full penalty of the law for what he - or she - has done. I am sure you will, as a religious man, want to help me all you can.'

The self-styled prophet seemed astonishingly unconvinced. 'God will provide. And God will punish. You should understand, inspector, that He is all powerful. Nothing happens on the Earth without His agreement. If our sister has been taken from us, apparently before her time, it must bc His wish.'

Ken lowered his notepad in surprise. 'Why would God want an innocent woman to be murdered in such a violent and horrendous way?'

His companion shrugged and smiled. 'It is not for us to question the will of the Lord. It is beyond our understanding. But she is not dead. She has gone to eternal life. She is in glory. And whosoever caused her demise will answer in full when the day of judgement comes unto us. His punishment will be infinitely more just – and far more terrible – than any that we, in our weakness and lack of understanding, could ever bring down upon him.'

'Or her.'

The prophet nodded. 'Or her.'

'At some time, when there are less urgent matters to attend to, I'll be glad to discuss theology with you. But for the moment, there is more pressing business. Let's start with your name?'

This was greeted with the condescending smile of a man who sees great things, who is close to almighty truths, and finds himself dealing with someone who is a but a babe in his understanding. 'If you think it necessary. Certainly. Though I cannot see how it will help you in your search. I am Brother Elijah, of the Congregation of True Souls.'

Ken had got as far as writing 'B' and then put down

the pad in disgust. 'Your Christian name, Your given name. Your surname. Your family name. The name you were born with!' He hoped that by repeating his demand in enough different formats, one would be recognised. It was at this point that Jenny joined them.

She intervened. 'We need the name on your birth certificate. For our records. We'll continue to call you by your preferred title of Brother Elijah if you wish. But first, your official name, if you don't mind.' She sensed that Ken was about to lose patience and judged that this would not be helpful.

Brother Elijah seemed more impressed with Jenny than he had been with Ken. He flicked his wrists dismissively as if his name was not of any great importance to him. 'Of course not, my dear.' He took a step closer to her. Perhaps because she had spoken to him more politely. Maybe because she was prettier. 'Forgive me, but I sense in you a spirituality, a closeness to that which is divine, even as you pay homage to earthly affairs. Seek ye the Lord while he may be found! May I lay hands upon you?' He raised both arms as if to bestow a blessing. He expected that this offer would be welcomed. The women he kept around him would never object to being touched by him. Anywhere.

'No, you may not!' Ken had had enough. He was, to put it mildly, curt. 'Name?'

The prophet turned to him again, with the

look one would give an annoying child who, nevertheless, had to be indulged. 'My name? My Earthly name? If it matters so much to you, it was Drake. Reginald Jonathan Drake.'

As Ken paused to write this detail down, Jenny jumped in. 'Tell me Mr. Drake: this woman that you knew as Sister Charity – were you sleeping with her?' Her boss almost dropped his pen in surprise. Reginald Jonathan Drake's face froze momentarily. When he responded, his tone was icy.

'The instruction from the good book is clear, young lady. Marry or burn. Burn in Hell for your lust, for your sin. Under our primitive marriage laws, the sisters in my charge cannot all marry me, if they need my companionship in their beds. But we are all of one family under God.'

Ken was still trying to make sense of this. Jenny cut to the quick. 'So you admit you were sleeping with her. And how many others?'

'I admit no wrongdoing. Am I a dog that thou comest to me with staves?'

'Possibly. And quite a randy one. How many women were sharing your bed? And did they take turns? Were some more favoured than others? We have evidence that...'

Drake decided that he had heard enough and interrupted her brusquely: 'I see no relevance in this. But you have your task to perform. I shall suffer your presence here while I must. Man that is

born of woman is of few days and full of trouble...
Job chapter fourteen...'

'He cometh forth like a flower,' added Jenny, not
to be outdone, 'and is cut down. Chapter fourteen,
verse one.' Drake stepped back, not expecting that
her knowledge of the Bible could rival his. 'It could
be very relevant, Mr. Drake. It could be that you
have set in motion so much rivalry amongst your
comforters – that's what you call them, isn't it? –
that one of your harem has been driven to murder!'
She glared at him, accusingly, as if daring him to
contradict her.

For once unable to bring an apposite quote to
mind, Drake turned away in disgust. Ken stared
at Jenny in amazement. Jenny's cool eyes took in
every detail of her opponent: this self-styled man
of God. The large, bushy beard, dark grey, tinged
with white. Fleshy bags beneath eyes that were
slightly watery and brown. He was taller than
Jenny by a couple of inches, but at least four inches
smaller than Ken. Leather sandals allowed his bare
toes to peek out at her and display an inch or so of
hairy ankle.

His nose was large and slightly crooked. His
mouth twisted slightly as he spoke, as if he had
suffered a slight stroke at some time, but it gave
the impression that he was sneering every time
he spoke. He wore a white mantel over a monk's
brown habit, with a large hood that drooped down
at the back. This, she assumed, was to further the

impression he wanted to give of being a Godly person – a prophet. But he was no Carmelite. No monk would treat women they way he did. Jenny was determined to expose him for what he was.

'We have witnesses who will testify that you have had sexual relationships with more than one of these women – your so-called sisters. We'll need to take statements from each one of them as to where they were at the time of the killing. This applies equally to you, Mr Drake. We'll also be taking DNA swabs from everyone here. Have you any objection to giving a sample, for forensic analysis?'

The hood swung round so he was facing her, and his watery eyes bored into her. 'Whatever. I have nothing to fear from you. God will be my judge, young lady!' Ken, shaking his head in amazement at the strength of Jenny's reaction to the self-styled prophet, left them and walked to his car to pick up a set of test swabs and plastic evidence bags.

But as he walked away, the man found his voice again. Jonathan Drake was not going to let this minor matter of a murder threaten his small kingdom. He had found his place here, somewhere he could be someone and be valued. He had struggled at school, but finally done well enough in his A levels to be accepted on a degree course to study religious education. This was partly because competition was very light. It was not a popular area of study and the tutors were facing possible redundancy if they failed to fill at least eighty percent of the places. However, the academic study of theology had failed to inspire him. The endless dissection of comparative religions, seeking out parallels and differences between Sikhism, Judaism, and Islam, he found amusing but ultimately pointless. It was in his obsessive immersion in the Old Testament that he found his true calling. Its darkness. The acceptance of a God who demanded total obedience and dedication, even to the point of asking for the sacrifice of your first born to prove your devotion to him, thrilled the young Drake to his core.

Here was a tyrant. Here was a deity who would destroy everything in a mighty flood if it had not worked out as He had intended. One who would destroy whole cities without a thought to the suffering of the inhabitants because they had disobeyed the rules he set for them. 'Thou shalt have no other Gods but me!' How those words set his young impressionable soul on fire!

His single-minded dedication to the readings of the Old Testament had impressed his tutors, but his lack of regard for every other area of study had dissuaded them from allowing him to complete the course. They had written warm testimonials to help him gain acceptance to one of the colleges that trained men and women to enter the clergy, but his passionate advocacy of Old Testament teachings and his apparent disregard for Christian teachings had come across at interview and rather alarmed the churchmen who were there to judge him.

Undeterred, he succeeded in gaining acceptance as a lay preacher in an Evangelical church. His passion and oratory were appreciated there, where talk of the coming Apocalypse and of souls writhing in the fires of Hell were received better than they would have been in the staid and secure middle-class naves of the Church of England. Soon he had built up a small group of disciples. As his hair and beard grew, so did their numbers, until he was ready to accept his true calling. Just as Jesus had commanded his followers to leave their jobs, their wives, their families, so he called upon the women (it was always women. Only women) who had recognised him as the next Messiah to leave everything behind and come to him. He had found this retreat where they could live and worship together. Some, it is true, had insisted on bringing their children with them, but he had been gracious enough to accept even their offspring into his family of enlightened ones.

But he recognised this policemen as one of the unsaved - a threat to the kingdom he had constructed and so an enemy to God. The woman with him, he could perhaps save. In truth, men had always seemed less enthralled by his teachings – but this was their downfall. His calling was more with the daughters of Eve. They trusted in him, recognised his special relationship with the

Almighty. More and more had come and put their trust in him. And their faith had been rewarded in so many ways. He smiled to himself. He had shown them that their bodies were a gift from God and should be shared. Sister Charity was lost to him now -but it was for the best. God in his wisdom had taken her. She had become too possessive. She had wanted him all to herself. And there was the other problem – the one he could not name.

All was well. He was in God's hands. He had nothing to fear. As the detective walked back to his car, Brother Elijah raised his hands to the heavens and cried: 'The souls of the righteous are in the hand of God and there no torment shall touch them. In the sight of the unwise they seem to die; and their departure is taken for misery. But they are in peace; for God proved them and found them worthy for himself! This is the Wisdom of Solomon!' And Jenny, not to be outdone, muttered quietly to herself, 'Chapter three, verse three!'

The patrol car was at the Durweston traffic lights when the call came. The driver turned on his blue lights and tried to cross the bridge against a red light. This brought all traffic to a halt as the narrow roads immediately became gridlocked. It took five minutes for three vans, a large lorry, four cars and a tractor with its trailer piled high with hay to reverse back slowly and carefully towards the village before the patrol car could proceed.

It was only five miles to Bishop Farthing, but it is impossible to speed along the narrow, winding lanes.

The driver was more accustomed to Dorset's major roads. Hardly motorways, rarely even dual carriageways, but faster and straighter than the narrow, winding country lanes he found himself on now. High green hedges lined the route, making it impossible to see far ahead. Pheasants ambled carelessly across their track. Round one of the blind bends, they came to a screaming halt, almost crashing head on into a tractor. The hedgerows gave way to the occasional thatched cottage, a picket fence separating it and its shock of pink roses or vivid, golden Hemerocallis, from the road. Then small clusters of buildings, tidy modern detached homes with tiled roofs and neat gateways. These interspersed with farmsteads that had settled into the landscape hundreds of years before and now nestled comfortably down into their gardens like broody hens pressed down on their eggs.

It took almost fifteen minutes to reach Margot's door. Annette had her arm around her neighbour, trying to comfort her. Margot was next to the pram, the blanket clutched against her face, sobbing into the cloth that still smelled of shampoo and baby talc.

Back at the retreat, Ken knew that to interview the twenty or so people would require extra personnel. He rang base and it was Geoff who answered. 'Hi boss! We went to the house in Winterborne but there was no-one home. We'll try again later. How's it going there?'

'Slowly, Geoff. There's a couple of dozen possible witnesses we need to go through. They're almost all women or children. Better send Gina over to work with Jenny on the interviews.'

'Will do, boss. She'll be glad of the break from typing up reports! Shame about the woman. Quite a looker!'

'What do you mean?'

'Nice figure.'

Ken paused in surprise. 'You've seen her?'

'Yes, boss. Didn't you know? Nigel from traffic posted the pictures on his Twitter feed. They're all round the station!'

Ken fought to control his temper. When he knew he was calm enough, he continued. 'No. I didn't know, Geoff. Can you forward it to me?'

Geoff suddenly realised he'd made a faux pas. For a moment he'd forgotten Ken's recent promotion – that he was no longer one of the lads. He tried to make the best of it. 'Oh, course. Now you're promoted you won't be on the general feed. Sure, boss. It's on its way!'

The phone pinged and Ken opened the file. There were pictures of the dead woman, naked, before the officer covered her with a blanket. And some highly inappropriate comments, along the lines of what he would have liked to do with her if she hadn't been dead. Ken was furious. It was not just the lack of respect for the dead that angered him. It was the attitude to women that underlined this. Was this man safe to wear a uniform? Would single women he stopped for a driving offence or helped at the roadside be safe with him? Ken knew that he had to report this to the Chief Constable and HR. It would make him unpopular with some of his colleagues, but he couldn't live with himself if he didn't tackle it. Jenny was walking up to him. Ken showed her the pictures. Her mouth dropped open in surprise. He was just about to switch off the phone when Geoff's voice burst through again.

'Boss! You still there, boss?'

'Yes. What've you got?'

'It's the man from the Bishop's office. He's just come through. Shall I patch him in to you?'

'Yes, thanks. And then get on to Gina.'

'Will do!'

A slight pause and then a querulous voice asked, 'Inspector?'

'Yes, speaking.'

'Ah. I was so sorry to hear about the death. So very tragic.'

'Thanks. We've got a few questions about the set up here.'

'Indeed. It is – how shall I put it? – unorthodox.'

'My assistant tells me that these retreats are normally for what? A few days at a time? But this group has been here for several months.'

'You're right, of course, inspector. But – what can I say? – we have had issues with the building. It was gifted to the bishopric in the early part of the twentieth century by a benefactor who made it a condition of his will that it be kept in perpetuity as a place of reflection and contemplation. A Christian retreat. But the upkeep has proved increasingly costly. You will know that we have very many churches and vicarages to maintain and as they age, the burden becomes greater and greater. Some of the buildings we have, reluctantly, to sell and this not only lowers the overall maintenance bill, the income from the sales helps with the costs of those that remain in our care.'

The speaker seemed lost in contemplation of the enormity of the problem. It gave Ken a chance to ask, 'So why haven't you sold this one? It seems to me it needs – I hope you don't mind me saying this – a great deal spent on it.'

'Indeed. And it is my office to juggle our dwindling finances in an effort to achieve the impossible. I would be very happy to sell the property and unburden us of it. But, unfortunately, the conditions of the bequest don't allow it. And so we are encumbered with a building that is gradually deteriorating and is surplus to requirements, because, sadly, interest in retreats has dwindled in our modern times.'

'So you were keen to have Mr Drake and his gaggle of ladies in residence for a longer than usual period?'

'Indeed. It was like a gift from on high. They've been there for five – almost six - months now. They pay a monthly stipend that just about covers the running costs and we understood that Mr Drake was a Godly man...'

Ken picked up on this. 'You said understood. You used the past tense. Does that mean that your view of him may have changed?'

'There is no deceiving you, inspector – not that I would ever wish to. This recent death is not the only incident that has caused us some concern. We've been contacted by the kindly lady who acts as unpaid caretaker. She raised some concerns about the relationship between Mr Drake and some of the women in the group. And then last week we were contacted by one of the husbands. He was complaining about the length of time his wife had been in residence when she had told him, initially, that she'd be away for a long weekend. We were actually planning an inspection visit in the coming month, now that Easter is out of the way. We are beginning to suspect Mr. Drake of building – how shall I put it?- a cult.'

'I think you were right to be concerned. Incidentally – may I ask the name of the gentleman who complained?'

'I don't think there is any reason why I shouldn't reveal it. It was – pardon me while I consult my notes – a Mr Metcalf.'

The husband of the dead woman! Ken made a mental note to follow this up and then thanked him as he saw Jenny approaching from the main door.

'I've got about half of them in the kitchen and half in the meeting room. At least I've managed to take the swabs. It's a nightmare, boss. They just keep arguing.'

A raised eyebrow. 'With you?'

'Mainly with each other. And the children are hungry. Two of them were crying.'

'Sounds like fun. I've asked Gina to join us so let's wait for her to get here. Meanwhile, let's get their names down.'

Jenny nodded. 'We'd best take their sister names as well, just to be tactful.'

'Whatever.'

'They take this sisterhood business bloody serious, boss. We'd best use their real names for the record, but call them their sister names while we're questioning them.'

'Makes sense.'

'Some of them are starting to trust us. They'll open up, I think. Sister Mercy understands we've a job to do. Sister Luke is no use to anyone.'

They both turned as a car swept down the drive and stopped with a crunch of gravel. Ken looked impressed. 'Must be Gina. She's pulled out the stops to get here this quick!'

But both of the front doors opened and two men got out. One was tall and clean shaven. He wore a dark blue suit. The top button of his shirt was open and his tie loosely fastened. He walked with an arrogant swagger toward them. His companion was smaller and walked with a limp. His black hair hung down, long and greasy. Ken stared at them suspiciously, thinking them to be journalists.

The arrogant one beamed a patronising smile in their direction. 'D I Jones? We were told we'd find you here. Weren't expecting you, though, love. With him are you?' He leered at Jenny, like a sexual predator.

Ken tried a swift put down. 'This is Detective Sergeant Grace. Yes, she's with me. She's second in command here. And you are?'

'Not anymore, sweetheart. You can take the afternoon off and make yourself even prettier. Then you can take my number and we can meet up tonight. How's that sound?'

'What?' Jenny was stunned by the man's coarseness. 'Are you having a laugh? Who do you think you are?'

'I.D.,' Ken demanded, no more impressed than Jenny. 'I asked for I.D.'

The man's smile got broader and he loosened his tie a little more to indicate how relaxed he felt.

'D.S. Cooper, son. Anti-terrorism. This is Baxter. MI5, Z Section. We're taking over. You're off the case!'

'From when?'

A nastier smile. 'From when, SIR,' he corrected. 'From now. Anti-terrorism are taking over. Hand over all your notes and any evidence you've managed to find. Then you're relieved, inspector!'

Ken couldn't believe what was happening. 'Anti-terrorism? Why?' Adding, very obviously as an afterthought, 'Sir. What about this killing suggests any terrorist connection?'

'Not your concern anymore,' then after a pointed pause, 'inspector. As I just said – you're relieved. We'll take over the SOC team. Now leave the crime scene. You're off the case!'

Ken was fuming but, outranked, there was nothing he could do. He stormed back to his car with the loyal Jenny in tow. 'Is he joking us?' Jenny was even more annoyed than Ken because she strongly resented her boss being humiliated like this. 'Terrorism? We're building up a case here. We've loads of leads. A jealous group of women. A prophet who's the son of Satan.'

'We've got their DNA swabs?'

'Safe in my car, boss.'

Ken turned and stared back at the two men who were lounging against their car and laughing over some private joke. It could be he was the subject of the joke. Or Jenny. That would be even worse in Ken's mind. He hadn't liked the way one of them had leered at her as if she was goods in a shop window. He focused on the issues at hand. 'There's probably nothing we can do. But let's at least check with HQ.'

A lady on the switchboard at headquarters apologised, but the Chief of Police was on an urgent call. She promised to ask him to ring Ken as soon as he was free. Ken cursed and Jenny squeezed his arm in sympathy. He called his office to kill time. 'Geoff? There's been a change of plan here. Can you contact Gina and tell her we don't need her? We've been taken off the case. I'll explain it later. But let's assume that I haven't told you that yet. And, thinking we're still running the investigation, how about you use your initiative and look into the finances of the retreat. And perhaps the financial affairs of the man who's running it.'

'Sure, boss. How long have I got?'

'Could be a day or two. I should let you know straight away that we're off the case – but I've been very forgetful lately. Oh – I've a call waiting – I need to ring off!'

It was the Chief Constable. 'Ah, Jones. Glad you called. I was just about to call you. Have Anti-Terrorism got there yet?'

'Yes, sir. They want us off the case. But sir – we're following a number of leads. I can't see how this can be terror related. I'd like to follow up on some lines of enquiry that are showing promise. This is a cult, sir, led by someone we suspect could be dangerous...'

'Drop it, Jones. It's out of our hands. Look, I'll share some intelligence we've been sent but keep this to yourself. Understand?'

'Sir.'

But Ken kept the phone on loudspeaker. He couldn't see why Jenny shouldn't hear whatever the Chief had to share. 'Military Intelligence picked up messages that suggest there's a targeted campaign by Islamic terrorists against members of other religious groups. We've already seen a similar attack on a synagogue. This unpleasant business in Dorset seems to fit the pattern. It's correct that Anti Terror take it from here. This is their area, Jones. Their expertise.'

Ken looked at the two fine specimens of policing and intelligence lolling against their car and smoking. He was far from convinced. Against all the odds, he tried one last time. 'Understood, sir. But I'd like permission to keep our enquiry open just in case the terrorism angle doesn't work out.'

'Absolutely not. This comes from high up, Jones. I need to be sure you understand me. We drop this and hand it over. Completely.'

'Sir...' Ken fought for grounds to disagree while Jenny sat with her hands clenched on sample bags, as if trying to squeeze the truth out of them.

'You're off the case now. Jones. And anyway, something has come up that requires your full attention. Losing this retreat business could be a blessing in disguise!' Ken steeled himself for news of his next case. He doubted it would compare with this. A missing sheep? A stolen tractor part? A shoplifter in Lidl? But when the news came, both Ken and Jenny gasped in surprise. 'I want you in Bishop Farthing village to support the patrol car that's just arrived there. It seems that someone may have stolen a baby!' Without a word, Jenny went back to her car. This was serious. They needed to leave immediately.

As the two cars drove away, a pale face watched from an upper floor window, a slight smile on her face. Sister Luke was glad to see the back of Ken and Jenny. She saw the newcomers, by their car, sucking on their cigarettes, but they had remained outdoors. They were no threat to her. No, it was the two detectives that she feared. They had asked too many questions and this had scared her. A sarcastic teacher at her infant school had mocked her when she tried to give answers, when she struggled to use half understood phonics to make sense of texts. The more she laughed at her, the more the girl had clammed up. For two years she had been a selective mute. She still had a fear of people in authority, that caused her brain to shut down and her mouth to refuse to work.

Sister Luke was alone in the upstairs room, as she often was. She had never been popular and accepted this as a kind of pre-arranged destiny. Her friends at school had been few and were girls no less bitter and resentful than she. There had been no boyfriends, although she desperately yearned for them. The attractive boys she lusted after ignored her completely. The only boys who showed any interest were too spotty, geeky or gauche to cause the slightest flutter in even a heart as eager for love as hers.

And yet she felt the need for companionship – for a sense that she belonged – and she had found this at last in the community of sisters. And their leader – the prophet – the bearded man who seemed to her so clever, so inspirational, touched with the divine, had lit in her a sexual desire so strong that it burned in every vein in her body. She was on heat, consumed with a fiery need for him. But she had not been chosen. She had not been one of his comforters, invited to spend night after night in his bed. No – for the past two months that pleasure had been bestowed on Sister Charity. To the envy of many, she was the one who spent the nights in the messiah's arms. Sister Luke was sure they were meant to become lovers and only she could bring the intense physical and emotional pleasure she instinctively knew he craved.

That harlot Sister Charity had to be removed, she knew. And now that she was gone, it was time to make her move.

Neither of the two officers had any idea what to do. They had both stared for a long minute at the empty pram. Sally was tempted to lift the covers to be absolutely certain that no tiny baby had wriggled down underneath, but the sergeant had warned her to touch nothing. They stood together, scanning the lane, as if a very small child might have jumped from its carrycot and rolled away. The windows of the small terrace of cottages opposite stared back at them blankly. The mellow stone walls were impassive. The thatch roofs sat secure on any secrets kept within. The roses that rambled through the garden were unnaturally still, as if sworn to give nothing away. A solitary starling peeked out from a crack in one of the walls, spotted the police car and retreated back to protect its young.

It was a warm day, but a sudden gentle breeze stirred the leaves of the oak trees and they whispered to each other of lost dreams and stolen children. It was in a language that only trees can understand. But the two officers shivered as the unexpected breath of cool air swept over their faces. They had phoned in. A bemused operator had told them to wait for back up to arrive. So wait they did. Time passed. They became increasingly embarrassed by their lack of action, as neighbours began to gather and ask what was happening and offer help. Sally decided her place was with the distraught mother. She tried to impress Annette with her efficiency by opening her pad and taking down a description of the lost baby. (Small and pink. White babygro with spots of apple and banana mush from the baby food pouch.) Meanwhile her sergeant got the blue and white police tape from the patrol car and sealed off the gate, assuring the assembled villagers as he did so that everything possible was being done and not to worry.

But he reckoned without the good folk of

Dorset and their intense sense of community. Throughout the pandemic they had looked out for each other, delivering shopping to friends who were without transport or were isolating; checking that their neighbours were well and had all the medicines they needed. Now, in this emergency, they were far from slow in rallying round. A retired policeman was quick to offer to organise search teams, but the two officers explained that they were waiting for back up and it would be premature to start searching so promptly. As the crowd of anxious neighbours grew and began to press against the police tape, they retreated to the shelter of the doorway and made increasingly desperate calls to headquarters.

And so this was the scene that met Ken and Jenny as they drew up – further from Margot's house than they intended because of the crowds on the road. There are no pavements in the village of Bishop Farthing.

Some in the crowd recognised the two detectives immediately and they were greeted warmly. It was only a few months since they had been at the centre of the investigation into the body found in the local wood. Many rushed forward to shake them by the hand, including Trevor the ex-copper, Sally Jones, Muriel the doyen of the district gardening club and Dennis, Annette's husband. Those who hadn't met the two before felt immediately reassured by their friends' reactions to the new arrivals. Ken made encouraging comments as he walked over to the two officers skulking in the doorway.

'How long has the child been missing?'

'About two hours we think, inspector. No-one seems sure!'

'Move the public away from the house. Clear the road for twenty or so feet in both directions. They could be trampling over evidence.'

'Sir. We tried, sir! They won't budge! They want to help!'

Ken turned to the worried neighbours. 'We need to clear the immediate area so we can check it for clues. Please follow the instructions of these officers so that they can form a perimeter!'

To the amazement of the two, the crowd immediately parted like the Red Sea. They rushed to their car, found the tape and began to seal off the section of road in front of the house. The road became impassable to motor vehicles. Within minutes they were fully occupied directing confused drivers to alternative routes that don't exist.

Ken turned to Jenny. 'OK. When we get inside, I'll interview the mother. If you can, do a tour of the house. With any luck, the baby rolled under a bed.'

'Let's hope so, boss. If she's been taken, we might never find her.'

Ken looked glumly back at her. 'Statistically speaking, if a small child isn't found within the first few hours, she's dead.'

On that sobering note, they opened the front door and walked into the hall. Jenny's experienced eye assessed Margot's home. The walls were painted a tasteful pale blue. No pictures, but a heart made of wicker was hung from a nail punched into the plaster board and LED lights were strung round it. The floor was clean. No sign of dust or of children's fingerprints on the paint work. But then there wouldn't be, with such a small baby.

They went straight into the lounge through the open door. Margot and Annette were sitting together, two cups of tea in front of them, untouched. Margot was snivelling and her friend had an arm around her, attempting to comfort her.

'Hello there. I'm Inspector Ken Jones and this is my second in charge, Sergeant Grace.'

Annette looked up. 'Yes. I remember you. You listened to me when I had a premonition – a dream – about the body in the wood!'

Jenny smiled at her. 'Yes. You were extremely helpful. You found the place where the shots had come from and identified a woman who helped us to solve the case.' She wondered if Annette would have any useful insights into this case – but first she had a job to do.

Ken tried to be as comforting as possible,

under the circumstances. 'I promise that we'll do everything possible to find your baby. We'll use all the resources that we have available.' He saw a worried look cross her face. 'And we can call on more from other forces if required. The first thing we do is to check the house to make sure that the child isn't somewhere indoors. Can we do that? It's just standard procedure so we can eliminate that possibility.' Margot turned her tear-stained face to him, saying neither yes nor no. Ken took this as assent and signalled to Jenny to begin the search.

She began in the kitchen. It was spotlessly clean. There was a steriliser for the baby's bottles and a tub of milk powder. She checked the cupboards cursorily, not expecting to find a child stashed in one of them. Again, they were exceptionally tidy. She breathed in. This was a woman who, it seemed to Jenny, was seriously repressed. To spend so much time cleaning and tidying a house – she needed to get a life.

Upstairs. The bed was made in the main bedroom. In a second room, there was a cot with clean sheets and blankets. Over the cot a toy was suspended that could be made to spin slowly and play a lullaby. On a neat chest of drawers, painted white, was a pile of disposable nappies. Margot had stencilled the baby's name on the wall over the bed: 'Summer'. Touching, Jenny thought. Spare clothes for the child were washed and ironed – nothing expensive, no designer labels, but all more than serviceable. No sign of a child. The smallest room upstairs was used for storage, but again was exceptionally tidy. Jenny checked the bathroom. She breathed in a sigh of wonder and was suddenly very anxious. She had an urge to rush home and spend a few hours cleaning and sorting it. If there was ever an unexpected search of her property, she was suddenly aware of what it would reveal about her. 'They'll think you're a right mucky, disorganised bitch compared to this!' she laughed to herself.

She'd searched everywhere. Except the loft. She gazed up at the loft hatch in the ceiling – dangerously suspended above the staircase. There was no obvious way to access it. And surely no baby could get up there?

As she walked downstairs, Ken was in the hall to greet her. She shook her head. He would understand. No sign of the missing person. She whispered, 'The baby's name, boss. You'll need it. It's Summer.'

Ken smiled. 'Sweet. Can you take some notes, Jen? We need to ask more questions.'

'Sure boss.'

'In cases like this, the abductor is almost always one of the family. Or someone known to them. It's highly unusual for a complete stranger to walk up to an unattended pram and steal a child from it. Especially somewhere as remote as Bishop

Farthing. We may have to ask some very personal questions.' Jenny nodded in agreement.

She took out her pad as they re-entered the living room and faced the two women. Ken's voice was still gentle. 'Do you mind if we sit down?' Margot shook her head. Once seated, the two detectives felt less threatening. They no longer towered over the others.

Ken tried to be positive from the start. 'We'll do everything possible to find your child, Margot. All the resources of the police force and our forensic labs will be devoted to that single task.' Margot did not look reassured. More tears rolled down her cheeks, unchecked.

There was nothing yet for Jenny to write so she looked coolly at their interviewee. Margot was wearing two halves of a lounge suit. To be more precise, two halves of two different suits. The top was purple and made of a flocked cotton fabric. The pants were dark grey, made of something slightly shiny. The shine was particularly evident where the pants had been worn thin, at the knees. Purple socks on her feet and pink fluffy slippers. Jenny was rather pleased to note that she took less care over her personal appearance than she did of her home. But Jenny was kind enough to grudgingly admit that the last thing Margot had prepared for today was a gaggle of visitors. No doubt she would have taken more care with her appearance if company had been expected.

Margot's hair was her most alarming feature. She had died it a striking shade of pink. Some time ago. Her scalp was now revealing the black roots that suggested that her natural colour was considerably more restrained. She had a snub nose and her skin, without make-up, looked ashen and slightly pockmarked. Jenny guessed that she had suffered from acne in her youth. Late thirties – possibly early forties. Jenny surmised that this child could have been her last chance to give birth, which made the loss even more tragic.

Even more sad, it was now clear to the detective that nothing mattered more to Margot than her home and her baby. The immaculate way in which both were cared for told its own tale.

Ken judged that it was worth trying to question her. She had sniffed and blown her nose. The eyes, puffy from crying, were now fixed on him. 'The baby's father – does he live here with you?' Margot shook her head and dabbed her face with a soggy tissue. 'It often happens that a close relative takes a child. Did he have regular access to Summer?' Another shake of the head. 'Could he have resented this? Wanted to take the child away from you?' Again a shake of the head and a blank stare. 'We'll need his name and his current address, so that we can check on him.'

Margot seemed to retreat into herself. She said nothing. Annette tried to help. 'Have you got his details written down anywhere, love? Can you just pass them to the inspector?'

Margot had a hunted look. She moved her head closer to Annette's and whispered. Her friend looked astonished and then gulped. After a second to recover, she half whispered to Ken and Jenny. 'This is awkward. It's a bit embarrassing for Margot, I think.'

Jenny sought to put them at their ease. 'Don't worry, Annette. You don't need to. We're detectives. We're unshockable. We hear all sorts of things. We never judge!'

Annette glanced at Margot. She had her head in her hands. They weren't going to get anything from her. She took charge. 'Margot told me – that it couldn't have been the father. He doesn't know anything about it.'

'About what?'

'About the baby.'

Ken and Jenny were silent for a second, taking this in. When Ken found his voice, it was with some embarrassment that he continued. 'Did he know you were pregnant? Could he have found out somehow? If he discovered that you'd kept it from him, it would be a motive for taking the child.'

Margot stared back at him blankly. Her world had crumpled around her. She was struggling to concentrate on what was happening. But Ken's mind was working overtime. An extraordinary possibility began to form that hardly seemed believable in the quiet village of Bishop Farthing. 'You do know his name, though, don't you? You know who the father is?'

Three pairs of eyes focused on the unfortunate woman's face. There was a deathly silence, only broken by the steady ticks of the clock that pinged like small pebbles dropped into a still, dark pond. Finally, Margot responded, tears welling again from her eyes, by shaking her head.

No-one knew what to say. The enormity of her confession was such that they sat stunned, taking in all the implications of her unspoken confession. It was Annette who finally rose to the occasion and came to the defence of her friend. 'Don't worry, love. These things happen. It could have been any of us. Just a one-night stand, was it? Men!' She looked pointedly at Ken as a typical example of the sex. 'Have their fun and leave us to suffer the consequences!'

Jenny's first thought was that this was unfair on Ken. But then she remembered their one-night stand and blushed. As for Ken, a small part of his mind was still at the Christian retreat. He could not accept that the victim had been the subject of a terror attack. There were too many possible suspects. And surely no terrorist would choose a retreat in the depths of North Dorset to commit such an act. Terrorist killings are always done, he believed, for publicity – to make the maximum impact. This one seemed too low key. No group had advertised the fact that they had perpetrated the atrocity.

So it wasn't surprising that he didn't examine Margot closely. She was suffering the loss of a child – a grief that is too great to bear. But that was not all. She could hardly speak. Deep in her subconscious was an anxiety too terrible to formulate – something that no one else in that room could even guess at.

Ken snapped his brain back into gear. 'Excuse me a moment. I need to contact headquarters to get as much additional manpower as can be spared. We'll start doing door to door enquiries. About what time did the incident happen?'

Still nothing but blank stares from Margot. Annette, however, was able to help. She butted in.

'Margot always has the same routine. Like a timetable for the baby. She always puts her out in her pram at eleven thirty. Then brings her in at one o'clock.'

Ken needed to check this. 'Is that right, Margot?' A nod.

'And I found her missing at quarter to twelve. I know because I looked at my phone. It was so unusual for Summer not to be there that I thought I might be wrong – that's why I checked.'

Ken smiled in acknowledgement and nodded.

'That's good. It gives us a very precise timing. Summer went missing between eleven thirty and eleven forty-five. We need to know if any of the neighbours saw anything suspicious between those times. Jenny – will you stay here and contact a family liaison officer? Margot will need some support.'

Jenny nodded and Ken walked back through the immaculate cottage and opened the front door, deep in thought. He went through in his mind every case of baby snatching he had ever heard of. There was normally a fairly predictable pattern. If this case didn't fit, it could work out very badly. If the child had not been taken by a relative or neighbour, she was almost certainly abused and dead. He breathed in the fresh air and tried to clear his head of these dark possibilities.

The road directly outside the house was now clear, but the crowd of people, now split between the two sides of the barrier, was larger than ever. Before making his call, he walked over to one of the officers standing by the gate. He decided this wasn't a job for Sally. He spoke to her senior colleague. 'There's something I need you to do, sergeant.'

'Sir!'

But you'll have to do it very discreetly. I mean it. I want you to look as if you're searching for clues. But go over every inch of the garden – front and back – and see if you can detect any area that looks as if it's been disturbed very recently. Understand?'

'Sir. You mean I'm looking for a – for digging?'

'Exactly. We need to know if a hole has been dug and something buried in the ground. But I don't want anyone to guess that that's what you're looking for. Understand?'

'You think that..? Bloody hell, sir!'

'I don't think anything. But we need to eliminate all possibilities from our enquiry. OK?'

'Sir!'

And the sergeant began to scour the lawns and flower beds, peering under bushes and moving compost bins – as if searching for stray clues that an untidy abductor might have sprinkled around. Ken called in and was promised ten additional officers immediately and more if he needed them.

But there was something the Chief wanted to check with him. 'I understand, Jones, that you've reported one of the traffic officers who was first on the scene at Marnhull for taking some pictures of the victim?'

'Yes, sir. And not just that. He broadcast them on social media along with comments that were – well – disrespectful to put it mildly. This is a clear case of grave misconduct in a public office. I assume he'll be dismissed from the force and put on trial. In previous cases, this has resulted in a stiff prison sentence!'

'Understood, Jones. Understood. I realise you feel strongly about this. But I want you to leave it with us. There's a lot to weigh up, here. Especially the public perception of the force. There'll be disciplinary action, of course. Serious action. But just drop it now, Jones. It's gone above your head. Understand?'

Ken was furious. 'I think I do, sir.'

'Good. Excellent. Good man. We'll get reinforcements to you within the hour. Keep up the good work, Jones. We have complete confidence in you!' And the line went dead.

Ken gripped the phone so tight that his knuckles went white. There was imperceptible creaking as the case dimpled under the pressure. Ken was a rational, intelligent man, but any abuse against women made him rage. If the force attempted to cover up this crime – this total lack of respect for the victim of a cruel murder – sending pictures of her naked body across the internet like some examples of soft porn – he would not be able to keep silent. And anger was building in him. The man at the retreat who was using all those women for his own satisfaction – he would not for a moment accept that the so-called prophet had any religious calling. He had gained some sort of power over these impressionable women and was exploiting them. And Ken had been taken off the case for, he was certain, no good reason. He was determined not to lose touch with the situation at Marnhull and when the opportunity came again, he would bring this man down.

But now the rational mind took control again. He went back into the house. 'Jenny. We're going to need a base in the village where we can co-ordinate the search. There's a hall, isn't there?' It was Annette who nodded. 'Yes. About half a mile from here. I'm on the committee. I can contact the others and let them know you need it. I'm sure they'll be glad to help – under the circumstances.'

'Thanks, Annette. Jenny – can you go down there and set it up? We'll need tables and chairs...'

'They're all there,' Annette told them. 'In a small room at the back. And there's a kitchen with hot water, cups, plates, cutlery.'

'And internet?'

She looked crestfallen. 'It's never been needed. It would have been an unnecessary expense.'

'Don't worry,' Jenny reassured her. 'We can install all the equipment we need.'

'Good.' Ken felt better now that a structure was being put in place. 'Set up the hall as the incident base and get the extra officers installed there. Let me know as soon as it's ready and I'll come down and meet with them.'

'Will do, boss.'

As Jenny whirled away to her car, Ken gazed sympathetically at Margot and her friend. 'Our liaison officer should be here soon, Annette. How long can you stay with Margot?'

'My kids are at a friend's. It's half term. I'll have to pick them up in about an hour! I'll stay till then!' She passed another tissue to her friend. Even though Margot was new to the village (she'd only lived there for a couple of months) this crisis was bringing them close. 'It's the least I can do!'

'Thanks Annette. Really appreciate it!' With this, Ken walked back outside and joined the officer still scrabbling round in the garden. 'Found anything?'

'No, sir. No sign of any recent digging. The lawn looks intact, and the flower beds are so packed with weeds any spadework would be bloody obvious!'

'Thanks anyway, sergeant. When the SOC team arrive, I'll get them to use probes just to be sure, but it looks as if we can forget the body in the garden theory. When does your shift finish?'

'Six, sir.'

'OK. I'll make sure you're relieved well before then.'

His phone rang. It was Sheila. He stared at it for a few seconds, unsure whether he should answer. It might be better to ignore it – pretend he was too busy to respond. Courtesy and his natural good manners won through in the end. 'Hi Sheila.'

'Ken. I've just found out you're off the case. How crazy is that? It's passed over to anti-terror. Damn stupid. This is no more a terror attack than I'm Bin Laden!'

'I don't think so either. But for the moment, for better or worse, I'm on other duties.'

'I'm supposed to report direct to MI5 now, but there's something I think you ought to know.'

'About the post-mortem findings?'

'Yes, But we can't meet officially. They've even made me sign the Official Secrets Act. But if we just run into each other socially, you know, just for a drink – and something slips out in the conversation…well. It can't be helped!'

This was highly irregular. Ken had been told to drop the investigation and with the secret service involved as well, he was on dangerous ground. But he was still angry about the way this had been handled. And if Sheila had truly discovered some new evidence, he wanted to hear it.

'Just for a drink then. Just two friends meeting for a chat. Where? And when?'

'Tonight. Half seven. The Lame Duck in Bournemouth! By the way – the case you've moved on to – an abduction? Of a child?'

'A baby. Six months old.'

'Taken from the house?'

'No – from outside. She was in a pram. Well, a sort of carry cot. On wheels.'

'Make sure no-one touches it, of course. Except with plastic gloves. And then have everything sent to the new forensic lab in Birmingham. They're brilliant. They can identify even single dead cells from people's skin. You'll be taking swabs from everyone you know touched it?'

'Of course.'

'Not the baby's obviously. But they can deduce her DNA from the mother's.'

'Thanks Sheila. Good advice.'

'Until tonight, then!'

And with that she rang off before he had time to respond. Was this a good idea? Had Sheila really got vital information on the killing at the retreat – or was she trying to worm her way back into his life? Well, whatever, there was no way back now. And if things got too hectic on his current case, he could always ring her and cancel.

As he put the phone away and made for his car for the drive to the village hall, he saw a woman duck under the police tape and head for him. Ken didn't recognise her. He was sure she wasn't part of the force and wondered what gave her the right to cross their boundary. She was smart. Black patent leather shoes with stiletto heels, black trouser suit with a very well tailored jacket and slightly flared pants. A white blouse and matching black leather bag which she opened as she approached. 'Detective Inspector Jones, I assume?'

'Yes. And you are?'

She whisked a piece of card from her bag and positioned it in front of his face where he couldn't avoid seeing it. It was a press card and identified her as Wendy Seymor, a reporter with the Dorset Record. 'Wendy. I've been wanting to meet you for ages. I've heard a lot about you.' And then she added, as an afterthought, 'All good, by the way!'

'I don't believe you.' He took her in. She was slim, about five six in height; brown hair cut to the shoulder, full and straight; brown eyes that matched the hair well. She wore make-up that made her skin look slightly granular close-up. But she was attractive. No doubt about that. But Ken was wary. He'd had too much experience of reporters' unhelpful interference.

She smiled brightly. 'I'm hoping we can work together. You give me the information – just as much as you want, no pressure – and I'll write the stories that will give you the coverage you need. Here, for instance – a child lost, isn't that right?'

'You need to liaise with our PR department.'

She moved a step closer and, lowering her head slightly, she looked up at him, giving him the full benefit of her appealing eyes. 'PR of course. But

I'm looking for something more. What shall we say? A special relationship? You've nothing to lose. I won't print anything you're not happy with. I'll have some exclusives, perhaps. You'll have a friend in the media who'll be helping you wherever I can.' One of her breasts was rubbing slightly against his sleeve. 'A local paper. It's read by over forty percent of Dorset adults. You can depend on our support. And we can help with appeals for information. Even offer a small reward.'

'I'm not sure. I'd have to check with my super...'

'Not really necessary, is it? We could have a private arrangement that would help both of us. What's the harm in that?' She looked straight into his eyes, held her gaze and smiled. 'They told me you're good looking. But you're even more handsome than I expected.' He felt himself reddening and for once was at a loss for anything to say.

'I'm not sure. I need to think...'

'Let's just try it. What's to lose? You can call it off any time if you're unhappy. But you won't be – trust me. Think about it. In an hour's time you'll have a gaggle of reporters here demanding your time. Nationals mainly – no use to at all. There's a couple of outside broadcast vans on their way now. They just want scandalous stories. This case will be a media sensation for two or three days. Then there'll be a government crisis, a celebratory scandal, and it will all be forgotten. But not by us.

I'll still be here to give you all the help you need.' She looked at him quizzically. 'Makes sense, doesn't it?'

He nodded, grudgingly. She gave him her card. 'Ring me anytime. Is there a number I can reach you?'

'I'll send it.' He tapped her number on his phone and waited till it rang. 'Just for now. See how it works. OK?'

'Absolutely. You won't regret it. Trust me.' She reached again into her bag and pulled out a Dictaphone. 'This abduction Ken. What can you tell me? Just what you're comfortable with,' she smiled.

'The mother's called Margot Watkins. Her child is Summer.'

'Nice. That'll get our readers' sympathy.'

'Good. She put the baby out for a nap in the fresh air, as she does every day. A neighbour walking past checked on the child and found her missing. She called on Margot to find out if she'd brought the child in early, but she hadn't. As far as we can tell the baby was taken within minutes. We're about to start door to door enquiries.'

'Perfect! I'll be able to report how swiftly the local police responded! You've given me the mother's name – what about the dad?'

'Not in the frame. She's a single mother.'

'Super! Thanks for this. It gives me a head start on the opposition. Now I mean this – as soon as you need an appeal for information, dashboard cams – anything – just ring me and you'll get everything you need! What about meeting for a drink tonight? Nothing extravagant – I don't have the expense accounts of the tabloids – but I can run to a pint or two.' She recognised that he was doubtful. 'Just for an update – to discuss what else I can do. I'm not trying to seduce you!'

Ken was desperately trying to process this. Could he trust her? She was right that he could stop the arrangement immediately if she took advantage of the relationship and published any details that were intended to be confidential or proved harmful to the case. His inexperience with the press was becoming suddenly clear to him. 'Tonight? No I'm sorry, I'm already meeting someone.'

She gave him an impish smile. 'Are you? Well, she's a lucky lady! Another time then. Let's keep in touch!' And with that she whirled round and headed back to the police tape before he could frame a response. Ken shrugged and returned to his car for the short drive to the village hall.

When the hall was built, it was probably assumed that most residents of Bishop Farthing would walk there. This was an odd assumption even forty years ago, because the scattered hamlets that make up the village are so far apart that only the young and fit can manage the journey by foot – and whatever you may accuse the villagers of, being young and fit would not be the first qualities to come to mind. The car park is a small area of dirt that could hold three cars provided the occupants opened their doors very carefully and were slim of build. Six police cars, holding ten burly police officers, presented a challenge that the car park failed dismally to meet. As a result, the narrow road beside the village hall, which had no pavement, had become both a parking zone and a hazard to oncoming traffic.

Ken found a space twenty yards away that he judged would cause the least traffic chaos and entered a scene of convivial bustle. Two ladies of the village had opened the tea bar. They were dispensing hot mugs of tea and plates of biscuits to all present, along with friendly smiles and cheerful chatter. Jenny had located from somewhere a map of the local area and pinned this to a notice board, covering as a result an outdated covid warning and an appeal for volunteers to help keeping otters from attacking a neighbour's fishpond. She had also opened a small storage room at the back and brought out a dozen or more chairs and four tables. Two men were setting up laptops on these and turning electric wires into trip hazards as they ran them across the floor to the two wall sockets.

Ken was recognised almost immediately and the officers – men and women – stiffened and greeted him smartly: 'Sir! Welcome sir! We're ready sir!'

He joined Jenny, calling out, 'Thanks everyone! Finish your tea! Meeting in five!' And then more quietly, 'Thanks Jenny, for getting things organised. I was held up. First encounter with the local press.'

She reassured him. 'It had to happen, boss. And it can only get worse. Missing babies make headlines. Losing a child is everyone's nightmare. But it's good that the local press gets involved. It's almost certainly a local who's done it.'

'That's what I thought. But I'm still fairly new to leading like this. When you're jumped on, and have to make a rapid decision, it's nerve wracking!'

'Trust your instincts, boss.'

'Easy to say!' And with that he called the team together, introduced himself and Jenny to those who hadn't worked with them before, and allocated most of the officers to work under Jenny, doing door to door interviews and checking for any CCTV coverage between the hours of eleven and twelve that morning. They were to ask if anyone had been seen – suspicious or not – walking along the road near Margot's house between those times. And had they heard any baby cries from a neighbouring house where they wouldn't have expected to? Nothing could be ruled out. Three officers he took back with him to begin a detailed search round the house, looking for any possible evidence of the abductor. Finally, one officer who needed the overtime volunteered to put the carry cot in the back of his car and drive it straight to the new, top of the range, forensics lab in Birmingham.

The search proved fruitless, as Ken had expected. When it got too dark to continue, Ken called it off and sent the team home with instructions to meet again at the village hall HQ at eight the next morning. He had promised to meet Sheila that evening, but it was now so late he half hoped she would cry off. But when he rang her, she was solicitous for his welfare. 'Have you eaten today, Ken?'

'I managed a few biscuits and three mugs of tea!'

'You must be starving! Look – I'm back home. I'll rustle up a pizza. Where are you? Blandford? See you in about an hour!' She rang off before he could accept or refuse the invitation. Half reluctantly, he turned the car towards the Bournemouth road and drove through the light evening traffic towards her apartment block.

The building was only two years old. It had a range of balconies overlooking the sea front. The cladding was tasteful, in two shades of blue to reflect the sea and the sky. There was a video intercom system. He pressed the button that was marked 'Dr Peterson' and a buzz immediately let him know that the main door would open for him. 'That was quick,' he thought. Either she had been next to the small screen in her apartment when he rang or she had been waiting for him.

The lift took him smoothly to the seventh floor and she let him in immediately when he knocked. Two impressions struck him simultaneously. One was how modern and stylish her rooms were. The other was how perfectly she was dressed. She looked fresh from the shower, except that her hair looked immaculate. She wore an almost white cashmere lounge suit that perfectly fitted her figure. Her welcoming smile was warm and the lustrous green flecked eyes dazzling. She took his hand to lead him to the dining area and as she moved a fragrant cloud of a very expensive perfume whirled around him.

This was so different from the only other time he had been there. That was a year earlier, when they had worked together on the body in the woods case. She'd broken the news that she was seeing someone else – having a torrid affair with her boss, almost twice her age. She refused to leave him for Ken, telling him that he would have to wait until the affair had run its course before they could begin a relationship – even though she thought she and Ken would make an ideal couple. Her calculating coldness shocked him. That was then he decided that – attractive though she certainly was – she wasn't the girl for him.

Her boss had moved in with her when his wife threw him out. It was clear that she had now rid herself of him and was, maybe, expecting Ken to take his place as though nothing had happened. Well, it wasn't going to be that easy.

The apartment was just as he remembered it. Much more luxurious than his humble starter home near Blandford. Two soft, white leather sofas looked invitingly comfortable. The carpet was thick and soft, just slightly off-white. Three of the walls of the living area were painted white. One feature wall had a modern and very tasteful wallpaper with a design of subtle, silvery leaves. Large sliding glass doors opened onto the balcony with its stunning view of the sea and the glittering lights of the promenade. He knew that she had used money left to her by her grandfather to help with the purchase. But everything around him screamed good taste. This was no footballer's wife celebration of wealth. He felt out of place. And underdressed. As had happened last time, he was at a disadvantage. He'd come straight from work, with no chance to freshen and change clothes. He wondered if this mattered to her. Maybe she enjoyed being one better than any man she entertained. Or maybe there was something about a man, rough and perspiring after a working day, that turned her on.

She poured two glasses of Prosecco and handed

him his. 'Drink up,' she breathed. 'No need to worry. You're welcome to stay the night...'

The two Anti Terror officers finished their last drink in the Sailors' Rest near Poole harbour. They were feeling good. They'd seen off the annoying young inspector who'd been first at the scene. They'd marked him down immediately as an inexperienced, over-enthusiastic graduate entrant. The kind that thought – like the young Morse – they were God's gift to policing, but were actually a pain in the butt.

They'd spent the afternoon supervising the SOC team in a search of the grounds. It, too, had gone well. They'd located the tyre impressions of a car that had parked just outside the Retreat grounds, where there was a convenient gap in the perimeter fence. Footprints led from there towards the spot where the victim's body had been found. Casts had been taken and these were on their way to Scotland Yard. When it was found that these matched up with known suspects – and they were certain they would - their job would be done. Now they had time to celebrate.

They asked the landlord where they could find women. He was suspicious at first, but eventually directed them to a street in the old town, by the dockside. Smiling lecherously at each other, they got in the car and began to cruise slowly towards the seawall, keeping close to the kerb.

Halfway along a dark street, with tall buildings each side which had once been warehouses and were now apartment blocks, they spotted the two girls. They wore short tight skirts that clung to their bottoms and hardly covered anything below them. Tracey had long dark hair that hung straight to her shoulders. Her eyes, black and shining, scanned the street constantly, looking out for both customers and potential trouble. Her skin-tight top, royal blue and cut low at the front, emphasised her small, pointed breasts. Her legs were slender, extending from short leather boots with inch high heels. Her make-up, when her face caught the light, was harsh, almost theatrical, to make her (she hoped) look seductive under the weak glow of the streetlamps.

Gemma was taller and plumper. Her face slightly puffy, with blue bruise marks round one of her eyes that the make-up failed to completely conceal. Although a little taller than her friend, her plump legs were slightly shorter, her top looser, her breasts more prominent. Between them, they sought to appeal to men with differing tastes. Some liked their women skinny, almost laddish. Others liked a soft full bosom and rolls of flesh. Both carried a small grip bag, containing condoms, their takings and a plentiful supply of chewing gum.

The two men eased their car up to the two women and rolled down the front windows. They said nothing, eyeing the two lecherously. Gemma was the first to respond. Taking Tracey's hand, she led her friend to the pavement edge and leaned forward to bring her head level with the window and pushed her bosom forward invitingly. 'Evening gents. Looking for a good time?'

DS Cooper breathed in deeply and eyed her lasciviously. This for him was one of the best perks of his job. The authority it wielded gave him almost unlimited power over bints like this. He grinned. 'How much, love?'

'Up to you, duck. Depends what you want. Thirty for a hand job. Forty to blow you off. Fifty plus after that, depends. You'll have a good time. Guaranteed. Whatever you choose!' And she thrust her ample bosom even nearer to his face.

Cooper put his hands on one of her breasts and squeezed it twice. As he did so, his companion made a 'honk honk' noise. Both found this hilariously funny. 'There's two of us, love. How about a discount, eh? Don't you do special terms for more than one? Reductions for coach parties, eh?' He smirked, 'How about it then? Suck one, get one free?'

Gemma spun away in disgust. 'They're wasting our bloody time, Trace. They want it for nowt!'

Tracey spat at them. It hit the side of the car. 'Bugger off! You're out of luck, mate!'

DS Cooper opened the car door and got out. Baxter

got out of the car at the other side. Cooper was smiling, dangerously. He reached into his inside pocket. Gemma thought he was going for his wallet and stepped closer. And indeed that's what the fold of leather looked like, until he opened it and showed his warrant card. 'Sorry duck. It's not us that's out of luck. It's you! You're nabbed. Get in the car!'

Tracey was furious. 'We're not doing nothing! You've got nothing on us!'

Cooper gestured towards his mate. 'He had his phone on the whole time. We've got it all recorded. All the offers. All your prices. In the car. Now!'

'What you picking on us for, you wankers! We're not doing no 'arm!'

As Tracey continued to protest, Gemma, resignedly, opened a rear door and slid onto the back seat. Cooper snapped his warrant card shut. 'Tell you what, duck. I'll give you a break. How about this, eh? If we let you off, leave you to get on with your business – if we do you a favour...how about you do us a favour in return? How's that, eh?'

Gemma understood immediately what this meant. 'We've no bloody choice, have we?'

'No need to get your knickers in a twist, duck. That's if you're wearing any! Want the deal, or not?' Fuming, Gemma shrugged angrily but finally accepted the inevitable and nodded. Cooper smirked. He'd known all along he'd get his way. He always had. 'That's a good girl. You know it makes sense.'

Meanwhile Baxter walked over and pressed Tracey against the brick warehouse wall. Cooper slid along the back seat closer to Gemma. He undid his belt and pulled his trousers open. 'Okay you slut. Dive in!'

She gave him a look of total contempt and then lowered her head. He grabbed her hair and pulled her face down to his crotch. This was what he loved. It was having power over women, forcing them to his will. It gave him the biggest kick. Proper relationships weren't for him. Too complicated. But this was all he needed. No chance of rejection. No smirking at the lack of size of his equipment. It was all about him and what he wanted. These sluts were just objects he could use for his pleasure.

When he'd finished, Gemma stumbled out of the car and spat into the gutter. Baxter had his hand up Tracey's skirt. 'Okay pal,' Cooper called. 'I'm done. You're in!' The MI5 agent took her arm and yanked her over to the car - then pushed her, sprawling, onto the back seat.

When it was over – and it didn't last long – the two men got back into the front of the car and drove off, laughing at their success in abusing the girls. But Tracey was determined that they'd pay for this. A new detective had made it known to the local sex workers that he would fight their corner if they were abused by their clients. She flicked open her phone and looked for the number she'd been given. There was the number. And there was his name. DI Ken Jones.

Ken leaned back in his chair and picked up his third glass of wine. The bone china bowl that had held the fresh fruit salad and crème fraiche was scraped clean. 'A really healthy dessert!' Sheila had assured him.

'It was delicious – really refreshing!' Ken was happy to admit.

'Cheese? Coffee?'

Ken nodded, but added, 'You said you had something to tell me. About the p.m.'

'Ah yes. The body at the retreat. I'm not sure I should say anything. After all, you're off the case, aren't you?' She smiled impishly. 'I should only report to special branch...'

Ken gave her a slightly wicked twinkle of the eye. 'But you promised. I hope you haven't brought me here under false pretences!'

'Ah, so you think I tricked you here, just so I can get my hands on your body...'

'Not in a professional capacity I hope!'

'Oh, trust me – it would be very unprofessional

indeed!' She lent across the table toward him and laid a hand gently on his. 'But after all – we're just two friends together, we've had a few drinks, it would be perfectly understandable if I let something slip...'

'Absolutely. No-one would blame us. So – what have you got to tell me? You said it was important.'

'It is.' She moved over and snuggled down on his knee. 'So, how are you going to wheedle it out of me?' And she put her lips on his. Ken had to put his arms round her to prevent her falling over. His heart was racing. For so long he had longed for her. But the way she had treated him the year before had cooled his feelings and now he was torn – should he take advantage of the situation – she obviously wanted him to spend the night with her – or be totally honest?

Another kiss and she began to tell him what she knew. 'The fatal injury was caused by a sharp knife with a blade at least six inches long...' She kissed again. 'Ah – you're forcing it out of me!' But when he didn't laugh, sensing that the game was losing any appeal it might have had, she slipped off his knee onto the adjacent chair. 'Okay – I'll be serious for a minute! First, the victim died as the result of a serration of the neck – as you already guessed. It was carried out with a very sharp blade. It cut through her windpipe and severed a main artery, which is why there was so much blood spilt down her breasts. Death would have been almost instantaneous. There was no sign of a struggle. No skin fragments or blood in her fingernails. She was attacked from behind and must have been taken by surprise. However, I'm sure that the assailant's head must have been caught in the back of her hair. There were some fragments that I've sent to the lab for analysis that must have come from his face and saliva.'

Ken was thoughtful. 'So this should give us his DNA?'

'Yes. Or hers.'

'Of course. Let's hope it's on the data base, but if not, we can at least check it against all the swabs we took from the sisters and their leader. The results won't come to me, will they?'

'They shouldn't. But I might tag you into the email, by accident of course. There's something else.'

His interest quickened. 'Yes?'

'She was pregnant. I'd guess about three months. I've sent a sample of DNA from the foetus to the lab as well.'

Ken was lost in thought. 'Was she? About three months – you're sure? She'd been there at least four months and hadn't seen her husband at all in all that time – he complained to the bishopric about this. So, it's someone she met at the retreat. I've a good idea who. Could this be a motive for murder? Had she become a problem – a liability?'

She kissed him again. 'There – I've told you everything. Now – time for bed!'

He hesitated. She was the most attractive woman he had ever met. At one time, he would have given everything for an evening like this. But after the way he'd been treated he was far from sure that she was the one for him. Beauty can be just skin deep. And could it be right to sleep with Sheila if he had doubts about their relationship? Was it fair on either of them? His head said no, but something – not exactly his heart – was most definitely saying yes!

Then his phone rang.

Sheila frowned at it. 'If that's a police call, wanting you urgently somewhere because some old dear thinks she's lost her cat, don't you dare answer it!'

But it wasn't. For a second, Ken was tempted to say it was urgent and get up to leave. But not tempted enough. He saw the sender's name and recognised her. 'It's not urgent, but I'd better take it!'

She pouted. A pretend sulk. 'All right. But don't be long! I'll be waiting for you!' And with that, and a sweet smile, she left for the bedroom.

When he connected with the caller, Ken heard a torrent of complaint from a very angry woman. 'Mr Jones? It's Tracey. You met us all and told us you thought we deserved police protection just like anyone else!' He immediately recognised her as one of the sex workers he'd met in Poole. But it was hard to get a word in as she proceeded to tell in graphic detail how the police had not protected them but abused them. He asked her to describe the two men, but he didn't think he knew them. 'Are you sure they were police?' She told him one of them had a warrant card and then remembered a name. 'Cooper! One of them said Cooper! The bastards've just driven off'

With a sudden jolt, Ken realised that these must be the officers that had so arrogantly taken over the case at the retreat. 'Trace – did you get the number plate? No? Look, I'll follow this up for you, I promise. But do something for me. They may come again tomorrow night. They're after easy thrills and I doubt they'll hunt far. If they do, use your phone to record what they say. Otherwise, it's your word against theirs – and magistrates will always take the police side. Understand? And don't worry – I'll make sure we're there in a plain car to move in if they do turn up.'

'Don't worry, if they try it again, we'll be ready for them!' And she rang off, leaving Ken seething with anger and worried by her last remark. Little infuriated him more than men using their authority to abuse women. But he knew that he would need more evidence than the word of two sex workers to get a conviction. He hoped he was right – that they would be so pleased with their easy success they would strike again in the same place, with the same women. He strode to the bedroom door to let Sheila know what the call had been about.

But the room was dim, lit only by a small bedside light. Sheila was lying in bed and the little of her that was visible suggested that she was naked under the sheet. She smiled at him and pulled the covers to one side, invitingly.

Sister Luke had waited impatiently for night to fall. With Charity out of the way, her time had come, she was certain. She had washed thoroughly and was confident that wherever the leader's lips could wander, he would be more than delighted with what he found. As a final touch – having no perfume of her own – she had sneaked into the bedroom of the dead woman and helped herself to some squirts of Alien from the bedside cupboard. After all, she thought, it's no use to her and if it had turned him on once – why not again? She smiled happily. She felt ready. And convinced that once the leader made love to her, he would quickly recognise – as she did so clearly – that they were meant for each other.

Her tummy fluttered with excitement as she crept from her room where the occupants now breathed slowly and heavily, sound asleep. It had been difficult to monitor the door to the leader's room. But she had done her best to ensure that no-one had sneaked in unobserved. She felt unsteady on her feet as she grasped the doorhandle to Brother

Elijah's bedroom. For a moment, she clung to it for support as her knees threatened to give way. She breathed now in short, sharp gasps. For her, this was the most important moment of her life. If the next minutes – hours – went well, as she knew deep down they would, happiness for evermore was assured. Everything she had ever been or known had led up to this. As she drew the door silently open, anticipation brought a pleasant wet warmth between her legs that made her tingle.

It was dark in the room, the only light coming from a single candle. But there was light enough. She could clearly make out the two figures on top of the bed. One, to her disgust, was Sister Faith. The other, Brother Elijah, was behind her, copulating. Like dogs, she hissed to herself. Like animals. Her right hand tightened into a fist of hate. If she'd held a knife at that moment, she would have plunged it again and again into the woman's naked back. That woman who was trying to steal the place that was rightfully hers.

They hadn't seen her. Fuming inwardly, she closed the door and returned to her own bed, plotting her revenge.

Ken woke from a deep slumber and found he was curled up against Sheila's naked body, soft and warm beside him. Her skin was satin smooth to the touch. He almost purred with remembered pleasure. But when he saw the daylight stealing through the curtains he was startled into full wakefulness. He checked the time on his phone. Already seven o'clock. And he had to be in the village hall to brief his team by eight. And the roads between Bournemouth seafront and Bishop Farthing were tortuous and slow. He kissed the nape of Sheila's neck. She was beginning to stir. Reluctantly, he pulled himself out of bed and began to pull on yesterday's clothes. 'Going already?'

'Sorry – sorry! I've got to go! Meeting at eight. Can't miss it!' She turned to the bedside clock and forced her eyes to focus on it. Helplessly, he blew a kiss and promised, 'I'll call you!' and then rushed from the room and the apartment, ignored the lift, ran down the emergency stairs, jumped into his car and raced through the early town traffic with his blue lights flashing. Cars moved out of his way as he tore along the A31 towards Wimborne and then sped up the A350, speed cameras flashing at him in all the villages along the route. There'd be no summons. Urgent police business.

He slowed as he took the road to Bishop Farthing – too many narrow sections and blind bends to speed – and arrived at the village hall (now, rather flatteringly, referred to as the incident room) at exactly eight o'clock and was greeted by a scene of busy efficiency. Jenny was sitting at a table at the front, with two chairs so that he could join her. Other tables held computers and phones. Someone had managed to patch up an internet link and ten officers were dealing with responses from the public. Many of the good citizens of Bishop Farthing had been up half the night trying to help Margot retrieve her lost child.

Some had been out with torches searching fields and hedges. No stone should be left unturned, apparently. Their diligence had turned up several black plastic bags full of evidence, all of which had to be trawled through. This consisted of innumerable fast-food containers, drink cans, banana peel, scraps of paper and cardboard, crisp packets, broken glass, rusty lumps of metal, one sock (inexplicable!) and two empty cigarette packets, both boasting revolting pictures of cancerous lungs on their covers. All of this was litter that had been thrown from passing cars over the past how many months, but, as the volunteer wombles were eager to point out, that car could possibly have been the one driven by the abductor...

Other neighbours had been following police advice and listening out for baby noises coming from adjacent houses. This had involved creeping out in the dark (concentrating on homes where they were almost certain there should have been no young children) crouching beneath a hedge and straining to hear any cry from a baby missing its mother.

It may seem surprising that these close

neighbours should morph so easily into sleuths, spying on their friends and acquaintances. But anyone shocked by this has not monitored the neighbourhood web site and read the comments and criticisms posted thereon. Posts that prompted one contributor to moan 'Oh, why can't people just be nice to each other...?'

The night-time spying had borne more fruit than the hedgerow searches. Three unexpected baby cries had been detected. But on further examination these had proved to be the mews of stray cats.

Ken returned the friendly greetings from his team as he made his way to the front and Jenny, but there was no mistake the atmosphere of concern that pervaded the room. Everything possible had been done on that first afternoon and evening, but in truth little had been achieved. A number of possibilities had been eliminated – such as the father being the perpetrator – but that was all. Ken noticed the white board that Jenny had propped behind their desk. Nothing made their problem clearer. There was no picture of the baby. Margot had not followed the modern trend of chronicling every day of a child's development using the unlimited storage capacity of a camera phone. And there were no snaps of possible suspects.

The only picture on the board was of Margot. Her striking pink hair shone from the photograph and rendered her unmistakeable, even from a distance.

He couldn't describe her as attractively feminine. He'd overheard one of the team calling her Doris and speculating that when she got pregnant it must have been a very dark night. He'd taken the man outside and given him a dressing down. Misogynism was unacceptable. And no-one should be judged on their appearance.

Jenny appraised him with a cool, detective eye. She noted the clothes he was wearing, the same as the day before. He didn't have the fresh look or the familiar aftershave she expected. She gave him a cheeky smile. 'Good night, was it?'

'Don't ask!'

Jenny looked at him questioningly. It seemed that whatever the gorgeous lady pathologist had planned, it had not gone well. But she was far too tactful to probe any further. Instead, she pointed to yesterday's copy of the local paper. 'Your reporter friend has done you proud!' she joked. He looked at the headline. 'Dorset baby missing!'

'Has she asked people to help with the investigation?'

'Oh yes. She's put out an appeal. But you must have made quite an impression!' Jenny opened the paper and showed him the continuation of the story on page two. She pointed to one paragraph and read it out. 'The hunt for Summer is being led by a young, handsome detective who last hit the headlines when he exposed a major drug ring on the South Coast! My, your fan club is expanding fast!' There were some sniggers from the back of the hall. Many on the team must have seen this already.

He blushed and waved it away, dismissively. 'It doesn't mean anything. It's just journalists – embellishing a story!'

'Shut up! I think I understand women better than you!' She gave him a reproving stare. 'Lots better!' She closed the paper. 'Anyway, back to business. She brought him up to date. 'There's a message from the forensics lab. They've some initial findings for us.'

'Great. Let's hope it's helpful. We need some good news! Put them on speaker phone.' He stood and addressed the team. 'Listen up. Jenny's just connecting us with forensics. Let's find out what they've discovered from the sheet and blankets. We may have the DNA of the abductor. Ready Jenny?'

'Just coming on now, boss.'

The speakers crackled into life. 'Detective Inspector Jones?'

'Speaking. What have you got for us?'

'We've analysed the DNA samples on the bedding and compared them with the two samples you sent us.'

'One from the mother and one from Annette, who

found the baby missing, yes.'

'We found two traces, but we're continuing to work on the samples. There may be more, but if so they're very faint. Of the two identified so far, we haven't found any that match the lady called Annette.' Ken and Jenny exchanged surprised glances. 'But there are traces from someone else and they are a very close match. At this stage, this second person would appear to be a close relative of the first!' Ken stared in astonishment at the loudspeaker. Jenny found her voice first.

'Bloody hell! You think that whoever took the baby is someone close to Annette?'

'We don't think anything. But the DNA sample you sent us – well – there's a ninety nine percent probability that it's from someone related to her!'

Ken's mind was reeling. 'It doesn't mean this was the abductor. Whoever took Summer may have worn gloves. These other traces could be older... But you said two traces – what about the baby?'

'That's another strange thing. We didn't find any DNA at all that could have been from the baby.'

'How could that be? Could she have been well wrapped up? And wearing a bonnet that covered most of her face?'

'Swaddled. Like a Native American Indian papoose. It's possible. But to get this lack of results, that must be how she was dressed every time she was ever in the carrycot.'

Ken chewed his lip, considering this. 'We'll have to check this with Annette – ask her what the child looked like when she was asleep in there. So the second trace was from the mother?'

'Yes. Are you sitting down?'

'No.'

'I strongly suggest you do!' Ken slumped back into his chair, bemused. The voice from the phone continued, with a slight Birmingham accent that made the next revelation sound even more extraordinary. 'The DNA you sent from the mother – Margot Watkins, right? The sample is from a male. Margot Watkins is a man!'

There was a collective gasp from everyone in the room. Ken's brain was working overtime. Suddenly things were falling into place. 'Margot' had said there was no father. That had seemed very strange – but not now. And she – he still thought of him as 'she' – had been so reluctant to speak. Maybe she had things she wanted to keep to herself. And her face. Now he thought about it – under the make-up – was, well, masculine…

There was a burst of animated discussion as the news hit home to the team. Ken got to his feet and the noise died down. 'Okay team. So Margot is a Tran. We're not going to condemn him. He deserves the same respect and the same service as any other member of the public. I hope you've all got that.' Nods. 'People can be born men and identify as women, we know that, right?' More nods. Ken surveyed them critically, looking for any sniggers or dissent. 'We're left with a couple of problems. The biggest is – where did he get the baby? One possibility – it would be ironic – is that he took it. I'm inclined to dismiss that for two reasons. One, we haven't heard of any other baby being snatched in the last six months. Second, if he was guilty of that, the last thing he would do is to involve the police!'

Jenny interrupted, 'There's another possibility, sir. It could be that he had the baby with a surrogate mother. That would explain his reticence. He wouldn't have been able to arrange it legally. Not as a single man who's a transvestite. He could have paid for it. He's facing losing his child and a great deal of money.'

'Thanks, Jenny. He's got some serious questions to answer. Our next step is to interview him again. So listen up. I'll go with Jenny to his home to sort this. Meanwhile, Len and Francis, check all the houses on the road for CCTV cameras. There must be some. These people seem very security conscious. We need any video from yesterday morning between ten and twelve. Got it? Sarah and Rich, stay on the phones to pick up any more messages. I want the rest of you continuing door to door, check out anything suspicious. We covered the immediate neighbourhood yesterday, but this place is a maze of lanes and separate hamlets and outlying farms. Block out sections on the map and visit them all, one by one.'

As they approached Margot's house, Ken was surprised to see the Family Liaison Officer standing by the gate, staring at the upstairs windows and looking perplexed.

'What's wrong, Trish?'

'No answer. Surely she wouldn't have gone out – she'd be indoors waiting for news, wouldn't she? She said nothing about leaving when I was with her yesterday.'

Jenny stopped by her side. 'She can't have gone out! There's a couple of dozen of us searching for her baby. She's having a laugh!'

Ken hammered on the door and turned back to the two women while waiting for a response. 'We've just heard some surprising news from forensics, Trish. It turns out Margot's a man!'

She stared at him in surprise. 'Didn't you know? It was obvious! Didn't you notice how she walked? And her voice? And the Adam's apple? I never said – I assumed you'd seen it already!'

'No! We were concentrating so much on the search we never looked closely at the mother!' He stared at the door. No-one had responded to his knocks. The house seemed deserted. 'Jenny – look in the garage – has the car gone?' While she obeyed, he tried to peek into the house through the downstairs windows. When he got to the kitchen, what he saw on the worktop filled him with dread. There were bottles and packets of pills – lying empty.

He threw himself against the kitchen door, but it refused to budge. He called Jenny. 'Any sign she's left?'

'No boss – the car's still there!'

'We need to get in – help me with the door!'

Jenny reappeared carrying a garden spade she'd found at the back of the garage. They wedged the blade into the tiny gap between the door and the frame. Ken pulled on it. There was a ripping noise. The handle of the spade snapped, but the door swung open. The sound created a ripple of excitement among the spectators at the front of the house who couldn't see what was happening at the rear but guessed that a breakthrough had been made. It was actually more of a break in. Most of the reporters had left the evening before, called away to report on new stories – from traffic accidents to house fires. Their editors were very conscious of the need of their readers and viewers for ever changing news-worthy events. Wendy, from the Dorset Recorder, had just returned, however, and she pressed forward against the police tape to be first to interview Inspector Jones when he reappeared.

The kitchen was empty. Jenny did not touch the empty packets of pills but checked them by sight. 'If she's taken all these, boss, we'd better be quick! Ibuprofen, paracetamol, antibiotics, anti-depression pills – Dozens of them! There's enough to kill a bloody elephant!'

'OK Jen – you check upstairs. I'll look down here!' And as he entered the living room, he saw her. She was slumped on the sofa, her legs splayed obscenely, and an empty bottle of whisky clutched in one lifeless hand. He ran forward and pressed fingers against her neck, feeling for a pulse. Nothing. 'Jen! She's here! We're too late, I think!' He called for an ambulance while Jenny rang for a pathologist. The paramedics had to be called even though there was clearly no chance they could revive her. Jenny grimaced when she was told that, as she expected, Doctor Sheila Peterson would attend.

Chaos broke out when the ambulance screamed to a halt by the gate; reporters, cameramen and curious neighbours scurrying aside to make room.

The paramedics were thorough but could do nothing more than confirm that Margot was dead. They left her as Ken had found her. Jenny waited for the pathologist while Ken drove the short distance back to the village hall. He wanted to let the team know what they had found. But more than that, he needed to ensure that they understood how much he was prepared to release to the press. It was, to Ken's mind, enough of a tragedy that she had taken her own life. He was dreading the idea that the additional news would break – that she was masquerading as a mother. That she was a he. It would be utterly disrespectful and callous for her death to become a media sensation because of her choice of gender.

He hoped against hope that no-one had contacted a reporter in his absence. He was sure there must be one or two of his team who had lucrative contacts with the press. As an afterthought, he rang Wendy. He confirmed to her that Margot had taken her life. Asked that she treat the news sympathetically. They were going to find any close relatives and let them know – then she could print the story. She was grateful and repeated her invitation for a drink that evening. He apologised, tactfully. He would be working. Another time he'd be glad to meet up. Satisfied, he entered the incident room at the village hall.

He assessed the faces as they turned to greet him. It was clear they had guessed that something horrendous had happened, but weren't sure what. Had any of them already been in touch with the media to leak the fact that their grieving mother was actually a man? He thought not, but he needed to make his views clear.

He spent a good five minutes emphasising the

importance of confidentiality before allocating new roles. Three of the team were set the task of tracking down any relatives of the man known as Margot and breaking the sad news of her loss. He felt a little cowardly leaving Jenny to deal with the pathologist, but she was more than capable and it meant he wouldn't have to explain for the moment why he wouldn't be enjoying her company that night. He had two ladies of the night to protect and he doubted she would either understand or sympathise with that.

Back at the Christian Retreat, matters seemed far simpler for the two officers who had taken the investigation from DI Jones in so peremptory a manner. Satisfied they'd garnered all the evidence they needed, they had called a meeting of the followers to bring them up to date. Brother Elijah agreed that his acolytes would join them in the meeting room. It was here that Detective Superintendent Cooper, with the secretive Baxter in silent attendance, broke their news to the assembled gaggle of women and children, with their self-styled prophet at the head.

'First, I've got to tell you that we are certain that the death of your friend, Sister Charity, was the result of a conspiracy by Islamic extremists to attack members of the Christian and Jewish faiths throughout this country. It fits a pattern that we've seen elsewhere of attacks on isolated groups with strong religious convictions. We've located the tyre tracks of the perpetrator of this terrible crime and followed a trail that led from the car to where your friend's body was found. All the evidence has been catalogued and sent to Scotland Yard for a full assessment. Accordingly, we are concluding our work here. We'll tell the local bobbies that the investigation is over and no person here is under suspicion.'

There was a murmur of relief, possibly surprise, from some of the cult members, but overall this was met with smiles of relief. Cooper continued, 'We'll be leaving first thing tomorrow to get back to the Yard to tie this up. In the meantime, let me say how sorry we are for your tragic loss. We hope, despite this, you can continue to live your lives of prayer and, well, spiritual harmony!'

The leader of this harmony bounded forward and took each of them by the hand, shaking it heartily. His eyes gleamed. 'Blessed indeed are the righteous!' he exclaimed. 'I see God's wisdom in you! Blessed indeed are those freed from suspicion!' But his thanks were accepted graciously by those who considered their work done well and were looking forward to a very entertaining evening before their return to London.

As the two officers left, Bother Elijah asked his followers to pray with him to thank God for sending two men of such wisdom and moral goodness to guide them in their time of need. Then he pointed to the sunlight pouring through the high window. A sign, he told them, that God was present and pleased. They should go out into the grounds, just as the Lord had sent Adam and Eve into the Garden of Eden to bathe in His goodness and endless bounty. Obediently, they stripped off their single items of clothing and walked to the door. Sister Luke was slower, watching Sister Faith as she revealed her nakedness. Evil thoughts swirled in her mind as she remembered the night before when she had glimpsed that same naked body contorted with lust, writhing on the bed with her beloved leader. She made a clinical assessment of Faith. What was it about her that had so tempted the man who should by rights be hers?

In her own mind, he had made a grave mistake. Her withering analysis of Faith's charms left her far short of Luke's own more worthy attributes. Her breasts were too pendulous. Her bottom too large. Her facial features – well. Maybe she lacked Luke's chicken pox scars on her cheeks. Possibly her eyes were larger, her nose straighter... Were these the superficial attributes that had led the prophet to err so badly? If so, she could put things right.

Sister Luke slipped into the kitchen and grabbed a pair of sharp scissors from a drawer. She was excited, focusing only on the plan that was forming in her mind – a clever strategy that would swing matters in her favour. Prove to the leader that she was the one for him. Mark out Faith as the unworthy Whore of Babylon she most certainly was. She did not think beyond the moment. She had no doubt her plan was true and just. She was about to right a great wrong that had been done to her and her beloved. He would thank her for it when he was in her arms, enjoying the passion that was theirs by right. And Faith would accept her fate as fully deserved when the leader explained to her how wrong she'd been to seduce him away from his intended.

Sister Luke clutched the scissors tightly and crept through the grounds, through clumps of shrubbery, past clearings filled with wild grass and buttercups, searching out her foe. The sisters had scattered. She came across them one by one, communing with God, praying, in the sunshine, kneeling naked or lying prostrate on the ground. And there was Faith – alone as she had hoped. She was standing next to an old oak tree, facing it, her arms raised to heaven, her eyes closed, her stomach stretched taut.

Silently, Sister Luke cut lengths of bramble, with long sharp thorns, and bundled them together, all the time keeping a close watch on her prey to be sure that she did not stray. A clump of long nettles nearby was scythed and added to the improvised whip. Luke turned back to the unsuspecting woman, still raised in silent devotion. It would be easy to attack her now, lash at her back and, when she turned, her naked breasts – but it was not enough. It was her face, Luke knew, that had tempted her true love away from her.

The nettles bit into her palms, the tiny hairs, trichomes, biting into her, sending histamine and serotonin surging though her, causing her skin to sting and swell. The effect of the chemicals filled her with rage. She ran up to Faith and screamed. As the sister turned to face her, Luke thrashed at her face with her bundle of thorns, lacerating her cheeks, tearing her eyelids, her lips – dragging trailing nettles across her breasts and nipples. Faith screamed in shock, pain and horror, but this only enraged Luke more, filling her with blood lust.

Brother Elijah was closer than Sister Luke had realised, just a few yards away. His time in the grounds was devoted less to prayer than to lecherousness and he had been admiring Sister Faith's charms when the attacker struck. He ran to defend her, pulling Luke away and throwing her to the ground. It was not the pain of the fall that hurt her. Nor the pressure on her wrists when he held her tight to the earth to disable her and then wrench the bundle of thorns from her grasp. It was his words. Words like stupid bitch, like mad woman, like bleeding idiot. They hurt. But then she gazed into the eyes of Sister Faith. Blood was running down her face. Her skin was torn in so many places. Revenge was complete. Her days as a temptress were done.

And Sister Luke was not going to be criticised for what she'd done. Even spreadeagled and dazed, she knew what was right and would fight for it! 'Don't you see? It's obvious innit? That cow was taking you from me! I'm the one you want! Not that ugly cow!'

The leader looked at her in astonishment. She lay on the grass, propped on one elbow, her legs apart, her naked body soiled with dirt from the ground, still clutching the remains of her whip of brambles and nettles. Her face, never attractive, was contorted with hate. He couldn't believe what he'd witnessed. He was unable to understand his part in it. Satan had entered her. He would do an exorcism. But first, he supposed an ambulance was needed.

Ken was fully occupied turning the events of the day over in his mind. Was he in any way responsible for Margot's death? Could they have done anything to make things easier for her – to help her to cope? He was slowly realising that she could not have faced the truth coming out, as it eventually would. When the public found out that the mother they had supported and prayed for was only masquerading as a woman, some at least would have turned against her. The hatred of her neighbours, along with the loss of the child, was too much to bear. She had taken the easy way out. Though Ken never believed that killing oneself was in any way a soft option. Those driven to it must be under insufferable, unbearable pressure.

And his main hope in the case was gone. It had seemed possible, even likely, that Summer's father had taken her. Not only was this the statistically most probable option, it was also, to his mind, the only hope that the child was still alive. If she had been taken by someone wishing her harm, then she'd certainly be dead by now. Too much time had passed without a word or ransom demand. He didn't want to admit this, but hope was fading fast.

But if Margot had been the father, there was still the possibility that the true mother had decided to take the child back. He surmised that this must have been a surrogate birth. The person who had carried the child for the full term may have had regrets. This was a strong possibility. There'd been precedents. They needed to find the biological mother. But if this was an illegal arrangement, and money had changed hands, the woman would have double cause to keep out of sight and be very hard to track down. However, more in hope than anticipation, he had asked Geoff back at base to contact all known surrogate agencies to see if they had any record of the birth – or any attempt by Margot to access their services.

And there was still the odd matter of the DNA

samples on the bedding that showed a close match with the sample taken from Annette – close but not a complete match. Who could it be from? He felt at a loss. For the moment there was little more he or his team could do. They needed a lucky break. Jenny brought up pages from the early evening newspapers, including the Dorset Recorder which had headlined its scoop of news of the suicide.

Ken could not help but be impressed by the local coverage. It was credited to Wendy Seymor, their chief crime reporter. The tag line read, 'Her Summer gone, a distraught mother takes her own life in a winter of discontent!' Beyond the clever play on words, the article was respectful and there was no hint that Margot was not what she seemed. She had agreed with Ken that it was important to let the first shock die down before any more information was made public. At present, the villagers were grieving for the loss of two of their own. It was impossible to know what their reaction would be when the truth about Margot came out.

His attention was snatched from the article – and a momentary daydream featuring the attractive reporter – by a call from Geoff back at base. 'Hi boss. I know that we're not on the Retreat case any longer – but I thought you'd want to know this!'

'Anything – yeah – go ahead Geoff.'

'It's from a contact at Dorchester A&E. There's been

more trouble, boss. One of the women was brought in around lunchtime with severe lacerations to the face and chest. They're keeping her in to treat her. May need skin transplants, they reckon. She'll be scarred for life whatever they do.'

'Are those loons from the Yard still in charge?'

'Yeah boss. But word is they finish tonight. Back to the smoke tomorrow. If we get a go-ahead, we could be back on it then – though it sounds as if you've got your hands full with the missing baby!'

'True. But if I can spare any time at all, I'd like to follow up at the retreat. Has she made any statement?'

'No. Claims she fell into a patch of bramble. The medics say she must be lying. They've never seen anything like it.'

'Damn. I'm sure she's covering for somebody. Fancy going down there in the morning – unofficially of course – and checking up on her?'

'Leave it with me boss. There's something else.'

'More? Sock it to me.'

'You asked me to check out the finances at the retreat. Turns out to be bloody interesting. The diocese charges Reg Drake, the fella who claims to be a prophet – five hundred a month for rent of the premises – and that includes all bills. But Jenny passed the names, addresses and credit card details of all the women to me. No idea how she got them.'

'Don't ask!'

'I won't. Turns out they pay him fifty a week to join his little cult. At least twelve of them. On top of that they take turns to pay for groceries. He's making more a week than he's paying the diocese in a month. Never mind prophet – profit's his middle name!'

'Good work, Geoff. It sounds like quite a scam. Is it illegal though? What could we charge him with?'

'Hold your horses, boss. There's more! I got a call from the solicitor for Jean Metcalf – the victim. He wanted to talk to you, but you weren't available. He was querying her will.'

'Will? She was fairly young to even have a will!'

'It had just been drawn up a couple of weeks ago. That's why he was suspicious. As a married woman it should have been straightforward. With or without a will, the house and any savings would automatically go to the surviving partner. But she disinherited him.'

'In favour of…do I need to guess?'

'No boss. Everything is to go to Drake, your would-be messiah!'

'So he's a lot to gain from her death?'

'At least quarter of a million. The insurance on the house means that the mortgage is paid. The solicitor is holding back – he wants to know more about the circumstances'

'So do we! Brilliant work, Geoff! Just on the offchance, could you check on the other women to see if any have made wills recently?'

'Already started boss. I'll get back to you as soon as there's news!'

Ken shared this bombshell with Jenny. The news was disturbing, and he felt torn between the need to track down the baby and the ongoing revelations about life at the retreat. And if he was honest, he'd formed such a strong dislike of the prophet Drake, and the two officers who'd taken the case from him, that there was a strong incentive to get back on the case.

Jenny agreed with him that it would be difficult to charge Drake with anything even though the financial details were so suspicious. But both knew that as a motive for murder, these financial details would take a lot of explaining away...

The afternoon was drawing to a close. His team was still tracing CCTV footage from the streets of Bishop Farthing. There wasn't much to go on. Despite the inhabitants' fear of burglary, not many had invested in surveillance cameras. The few that were operational had borne mixed results. No prowler could be seen approaching Margot's – or any other – house. The only activity seemed to be children playing nearby. It had been a half term holiday. During the hour under investigation, some vehicles had driven past. They were mainly delivery vans from large supermarkets or courier companies. Each one was being checked. It was taking time. But there were, worryingly, no other leads to follow. Jenny had asked Annette about the unusual DNA traces. They were not Annette's but seemed to be from someone closely related to her. She had no idea who this could be and it looked like a false trail.

Ken and Jenny left two of the team to hold the fort on night duty and set off for Poole. There was still the matter of the two officers who had assaulted the ladies of the night. And these were two pieces of scum that Ken was hoping against hope would try their luck again tonight. And this time he'd be waiting for them.

Perhaps there'd been an understanding that Ken would spend the night with Sheila again, but nothing had actually been said. He took the coward's way out. Assuming she would still be working on Margot's post-mortem, he sent her a text explaining that he was working that evening and would be so late he had better spend what was left of the night at home. He hoped she'd understand.

He wondered if she would. He felt guilty, of course. Did she understand why he felt so bad about the way she'd treated him? He thought not. To her, it probably seemed the sensible way to proceed. She was having an affair with her boss. She had increasing doubts about him. He was too old for her, too possessive, too married and too snipped. The operation he had volunteered for, when still with his first wife, to ensure he couldn't make her pregnant again, meant that if Sheila stayed with him there was no possibility of children. And she had begun to have strong feelings for Ken, as he had for her. But she had been slow to take action. She expected Ken to stay away and wait, while she was still having an affair with her boss, until she was ready to end it.

And when she finally did, her boss had turned up at her door with a suitcase claiming his wife had found about their affair and turned him out. And she'd believed him. And allowed him to move in. This had been the final humiliation for Ken – more than he could bear. He'd sworn to put her out of his life – and heart – for ever. And now, with female cunning, she was trapping him again.

The problem was, he was still strongly attracted to her. He hated himself for giving in to his desire for her, but surrender he had. For one night. His head told him it had to be his last. His heart (and other parts of him) were pulling him back towards her, despite everything. Would she respond to his text?

In case she did, he switched off his phone.

There was some time to kill before the pubs closed. This was when the two officers had made their move on Tracey and Gemma previously so, if Ken and Jenny were to catch them, they had at least two hours to kill. He pulled up outside the burger bar off the A31 on the way into Poole centre. 'We've got time to kill. And we need something to eat. Choose what you like. It's on me!'

'Oh my God! You certainly know how to spoil a girl! I bet this isn't where you take all your conquests!' she smiled, teasingly. Ken nodded in acknowledgement. A wave of guilt swept over him. The word 'conquest' had hit hard. Is that how she saw it? Two Christmases ago, after a team get-together at a pub, they had shared a taxi. When they reached Jenny's flat she'd invited him in for a coffee and they had ended up spending the night together. It had never been mentioned again by either of them. They had both been a little drunk and he had dismissed it as just one of those things. A one night stand they should put behind them, especially as they worked on the same team. Romantic entanglements between serving officers were frowned upon. He'd sort of assumed that she felt the same. But did she? Or was there a hidden message in that last remark? Did she feel she had become another conquest? Another woman ticked off in a line of seductions? That would be so untrue.

He respected Jenny. He tried to treat all women with respect but Jenny – she was such a valued colleague. So often, her insights had been a major factor in solving a case. Just look at how rapidly she had seen through Drake and recognised that he was a sexual predator, preying on the so-called sisters in his charge. No – he held Jenny in the highest professional regard. And he liked her very much as a person. He was mortified to think that she might have spent the last two years secretly believing that he was no better than Drake.

For a long second he was silent, taking in the implications of all this and stuck for anything to say. Jenny wasn't sure why he was staring at her, slightly strangely. Something had touched a raw nerve, but she wasn't sure what or why. 'A salad then. And fruit juice. I'm on a health kick!'

'Oh. I've brought you to the wrong place then, haven't I?'

'No, it's fine.'

He got the orders, and they ate in silence. Ken wanted very much to talk about all that was going through his mind but was afraid to start. It was certain to be a very delicate and awkward conversation and somehow the burger place's carpark didn't seem to have the right ambience.

Jenny picked at her salad, deep in thought. That night two years ago had meant a lot to her. He was only the second man she'd slept with, and it had been - well – wonderful. He'd been so strong and yet so gentle. She idolised Ken. He was intelligent, caring, empathetic. He respected women and detested men who took advantage of them. She had been tipsy but remembered every detail of their love making. When he slipped away in the morning to get home and change, she had lain in bed and dreamed. In her fantasy world, this had been just the beginning of their relationship. She would cook for him, care for him, love him for ever. But the next time she saw him, it was as if nothing had happened. He had never mentioned their night together and she had assumed, eventually, that he had put it behind him. She had accepted that their relationship would always be as inspector and sergeant on the same team. And if that was all it would ever be, she would gladly settle for that. She wanted to be near him. To be his right hand. It was enough.

A bitter smile. Almost enough.

Because he had set the bar too high. She'd turned thirty. Aware of time passing, she'd looked at other men. Other men on the team. Ones she met occasionally in the company of friends. She'd even scrolled through a dating site. Worth trying, she supposed. But she had no enthusiasm for it. Compared with Ken – well.

They deposited the wrappers in litter bins near the car, trying to ensure that the correct wrapping went in the right recycling container. Still without speaking they set off for the harbour, Jenny wiping her fingers on the stiff, barely absorbent tissue provided with the meal. They negotiated a large, confusing roundabout and weaved down narrow streets to where the old warehouses towered into the dark sky.

Twenty yards away, they could see two figures, tucked into the shelter of a doorway. Ken squinted at them. It was hard to make out in the dark, but this was where Tracey and Gemma had said they would be. He turned to Jenny. 'I'll go out and check on them. Remind them to use their phones to record if Baxter and Cooper turn up again.' She nodded. There seemed to be a distance between them far greater than the width of the car. She was regretting the silly joke she had made. But their friendship was strong and went back over three years now. She was hoping they'd get a chance to talk through what had happened two Christmases ago. It was time they did, she thought. They should never have just ignored it.

He unwrapped himself from the car. He was so tall and lithe that he never simply got out. She watched him walk down the narrow, dimly lit street. Some windows, narrow and high, were lit. As he passed beneath them, light fell on the top of his head. His full hair, brown in daylight, shone orange, then green, then a pale shade of blue, according to the hue coming from each bulb as he progressed towards the young women. She felt fiercely protective and followed him closely with her eyes.

Clearly, these women were Tracey and Gemma. She saw them recognise him and move forward, obviously pleased that he was there. A brief conversation. Vigorous nods. Then Ken spun round and returned to the car.

'The two scumbags haven't turned up yet. We shouldn't have long to wait, unless they've opted for an early night.'

'Unlikely, boss. Men like them want easy sex and once they've found it, they'll come for it again.'

'Let's hope so. Tracey knows what to do. But they told their minders what happened in case we didn't turn up. I can't see them though.'

They both peered through the windscreen into the darkness. Ken had switched off the lights in the car so anyone passing would think it empty. The warehouses seemed to have crept closer together. They were built of stone from nearby Purbeck, but it had blackened over time, coated with soot from the furnaces of the steam ships that had once tied up nearby. The silence was almost complete, except for the regular rhythm of boats creaking in the marina as they were rocked by the incoming waves of the tide.

Jenny closed her eyes momentarily. Always before, alone in the car with Ken, she had felt at ease – comforted. But tonight felt strangely different. It was time to say something – anything – to clear the air. She couldn't leave it like this any longer. She opened her eyes and turned to look at him – was about to speak – when he pushed her down with his left arm. 'Duck down!' They both slid down in their seats so their heads were low. As they did so, the lights from an oncoming car shone brightly into theirs through the rear screen. Then the car swept past them, squealing to a halt alongside the two sex workers.

They were too far away to hear what was being said, but it was obvious that an animated conversation was taking place. Again, Cooper flashed his warrant card and then took Gemma's arm and pulled her towards one of the rear doors of the car. Baxter pushed Tracey into the doorway and began to grope her. Jenny reached for the door handle ready to intervene. Ken put his hand on her arm to delay her. He could see two figures emerging from the darkest part of the street. They approached stealthily to avoid detection. Baxter and Cooper were too occupied with the young women to see them. Jenny gasped as the two strangers passed under a lighted window. They were swinging baseball bats as they walked.

'Boss! Can you see what they're carrying?'

Ken smiled grimly. 'They've committed no offence yet – not like those effing excuses for guardians of the law! We'll have to wait. If we see them using the weapons, then of course we'll intervene. Eventually. But it's only right that we don't interfere until they're plainly guilty of some misdemeanour. It's a free country after all!' He settled back to watch. He thought these men deserved a good thrashing. He just wished he could have done it himself.

Jenny stared at him anxiously. She would stick by him no matter what, but her heart was beating hard. This could get very nasty. Baxter had his back to the men as they neared him. Cooper must have been fully occupied too. There was no reaction from him inside the car as one of the men reached it and grasped the door handle.

When it happened the two men acted as one. Baxter was pulled back and, taken by surprise, fell into the gutter. His assailant lifted his baseball bat and cracked it across the agent's back. It made a sharp noise in the quiet of the night like something breaking. The other attacker yanked open the car door and grabbed Cooper by the hair. He pulled him from the car so that he fell hard onto the tarmac, sprawled across the road. He was half naked and the bat came down on his bare thighs. There was a scream of pain. Calmly, Ken opened the door of their car and he and Jenny got out, but again Ken restrained Jenny so that she wouldn't walk too quickly to the fracas.

Baxter was being kicked in the stomach and then the baseball bat cracked him across the skull. All signs of struggle stopped. His assailant began removing the agent's clothing. Cooper was trying to defend himself from a rain of blows onto the body. Crack after crack sounded out the breaking of ribs. Jenny could hold back no longer. 'Stop! Police!'

The two assailants looked up, saw that Ken and Jenny were still some distance away and seemed to slash at their victims before running. Ken broke into a trot, calling to Jenny to call an ambulance and police back-up. She had to slow down to do it. When she reached the scene, Baxter was unconscious. Cooper was still awake but writhing on the ground in agony. Blood was spilt on the road. Ken saw that it had come from both men.

Ken helped Gemma from the car as Jenny reached them and cried in horror, 'My God! Look what the bastards have done!'

Ken made no comment. He gripped Gemma's arm. 'Did you get it recorded?' She nodded, staring at the two men who had so abused them, now helpless and bleeding on the pavement. She was no more sympathetic than Ken. 'Bloody deserved it an all! Told you our fellas would give them a hiding!'

Ken looked her in the eye. 'You never told me anything, remember? And you've no idea who those men were. Get that straight. Listen – have you ever seen those men who beat these officers up? Have you?'

Gemma grinned slyly. 'Me? Never. Never seen'em.

Too dark, wontit?'

Cooper stirred. 'That's Jones, isn't it? Why didn't you stop them? You could have stopped them!'

'Sorry, sir. We came as soon as we could. My sergeant here called out as soon as we saw them. That's when they ran off! She probably saved your life.' Cooper was moaning in considerable pain. Baxter was still lifeless.

'Get an ambulance, damn you!'

'One's on its way sir. But while we wait, I need to tell, you that I'm arresting you for gross abuse of public office, misuse of your office for sexual gain. You don't need to say anything, but anything you do say...'

'Are you mad? You should be chasing after the thugs who attacked us!'

'We will of course put together as full a description as we can of your assailants. However, you chose to do your business in such a dark location that it may well be impossible to identify them. Meanwhile, you'll be taken to hospital under guard and transferred to the local nick as soon as the medical staff tell us you can be moved.'

Cooper's face twisted with fury. 'You've no grounds! You try to go through with this and you'll be back on the beat, Jones. It's the end of your career, you hear me!'

'You were using your authority as officers of the

law to force these young women to engage in sexual acts with you. It's gross misconduct. It's your careers that are over, not mine.'

'You'll never make it stick! Our word against the lies of a couple of whores! There's not a magistrate in the country who won't laugh you out of court!'

'Maybe not. These young ladies have mobile phones. It wouldn't surprise me to find out that they recorded every word you said to them.'

'You lump of shite!'

Then the blue lights of the ambulance shed an eerie light on the scene, turning the blood a deep shade of black.

The next morning – a Saturday – Annette was in her kitchen clearing the breakfast pots when there was a gentle knocking at the door. It was two schoolfriends of her daughter Emma. She looked down at them, their blonde hair and wide eyes. They were staring up at her, clearly excited. 'We've come for Emma!'

'To play!'

'Is she up yet?'

'We want to see her new baby!'

Annette gazed down, puzzled. She hadn't bought Emma a new doll since her birthday months ago.

'She's cleaning her teeth. She'll be down in a sec.'

Should she ask? It would be on her mind all day if she didn't. 'New baby? Where she get that from?' Annette gave a false laugh. 'I didn't know she'd got a new doll!'

The two friends' expression changed, as if they suddenly realised they'd said too much. 'No missus. Course not. We got mixed up. We'll wait. By gate!' And they turned on their heels and ran towards the garden fence before she could quiz them further. Annette stood stock still. Her stomach churned and a cold hand seemed to grip her heart, stopping it from beating for a chilling second. Baby? A wave of panic swept over her. It couldn't be, surely? And if it was – where could it be?

She shouted up the stairs, 'Emm! Down here! Now!' Then turned back to the kitchen door. At the bottom of the garden Emma's friends had stopped, huddled by the small shed that her daughter sometimes used as a den. Annette's knees almost buckled with the horror of what might have happened. Had Emma taken the baby? What had the detectives said? Traces of DNA on the cot sheets – not hers – but someone close to her – someone from the same family? It couldn't be, surely? It was too terrible to even contemplate...

'EMM! Here now!'

A frightened face appeared at the door that led to the lounge and the staircase. Her daughter looked pale and frightened. She didn't want to get too near. She could tell her mum was very angry. And Emma's conscience was far from clear.

Annette fought to retain her balance. Then she lunged forward, grabbed Emma by her T-shirt and pushed her against the fridge, keeping her pinned there so that she could carry out an interrogation.

'They've come to see your new baby!' She waved her hand in the direction of the shed. 'Tell me the truth now, Emma! You know I'll know if you're lying, don't you?' Emma nodded, terrified. Yes. She knew that her mum had the gift. She could tell who was lying. She'd proved it again and again. 'What have you got in that shed? Eh? The truth now!'

Tears began to swell from the little girl's eyes. She turned her head one way, then the other. No, there was no escape.

'Tell me, Emma - or heaven help me I'll give you such a hiding!' She pushed a hand against the child's chest, pressed her against the door of the fridge and lowered her head so that her own eyes were level with Emma's. 'Have you got a baby? Don't tell me there's a baby!' Emma didn't, grateful for what seemed a way out. But it didn't last. 'Tell me! Now! Is there a baby in that bloody shed?' Emma nodded, dumbly.

Annette was facing the worst day of her life. 'How could you? When everyone was searching! Did you take her? I don't believe you! I don't believe it!' She dragged the child by her elbow out into the garden, down the long path to the broken-down garden shed. She yelled at the two girls cowering under the magnolia. 'Have you seen her? The baby?' They nodded, too frightened to speak. Now the most dreadful question. She had to ask it. But three days had passed. Had they fed her? Where had they got milk? Was she still alive?

'The baby! Tell the truth! Is she crying? Is she...?' It was almost too awful to ask: 'Is she moving?'

The girls stared at her uncomprehending. Then, slowly, they shook their heads.

Annette moved closer and stared through the shed door into the dimness of the interior. She saw a crate that had been turned into a makeshift crib. She saw a bundle of cloth, comfort cloths, blankets. Everything was silent and – chillingly - still. Her worst fears were realised. Why hadn't she felt something before? Her intuition – her second sight her friends called it – was normally so reliable and on this one occasion, when it was so necessary, she'd felt nothing! She looked at the little body stiff and lifeless.

No longer angry. Beyond anger. Incredibly sad. 'What were you thinking Emm? How could you do it?'

Ken stared at the message on his phone. It was from Sheila. The post-mortem on Margot established that she'd died from a massive overdose of pain killers, barbiturates, and alcohol. She'd been gone at least four hours before they found her. The pathologist confirmed there was nothing more they could have done.

But Ken still felt more than a trace of guilt. He had pleaded he had too much to do to attend and had arranged for another officer to attend the p.m. Further, obsessed with the baby and with so much of the Christian retreat investigation still on his mind, the possibility that Margot was born a man had never occurred to him. If he had realised how much shame she was facing, how much respect from her neighbours she was afraid of losing along with the loss of the child, he would have put in extra support for her. Psychiatric involvement at least and someone with her at all times.

And progress was grinding to a halt. All the drivers had been traced and none of them was outside Margot's at the time the baby was taken. All had perfectly good alibis. Their deliveries were timed and backed up with photographs of the packages at doorsteps or in the hands of their recipients. They weren't back at square one, he thought grimly, they were stuck at square one. They'd never left it. It was the first case he'd ever handled that was just going nowhere. And there'd been a rider to Sheila's message, asking when they'd meet up again. What was he to say?

It couldn't get worse. But then it did.

A call came through from his line manager and he didn't sound happy. "Jones! What in God's name were up to last night?'

'There was a fracas in Poole. Sir.'

'I know. Two male officers were badly beaten – one in hospital still unconscious!'

'Yes sir. We were able to intervene and prevent further hurt.'

'And then you let the two attackers get away and arrested the two officers who were beaten up! Are you crazy? Detective Superintendent Cooper has filed a complaint against you!'

'I've requested the local police search for the men involved, sir. I felt our priority was to get urgent medical help for the two officers who seemed to be seriously injured.'

'Luckily, the locals have already traced the two sex workers and so I think it will be easy to track them down.' Ken doubted it. 'But the arrests, Jones. Bloody stupid!'

'Gross abuse of public office, sir.'

'I bloody know what you bloody charged them with! It won't stick, Jones! It's just the women's word against theirs! No magistrate will take them seriously! They've both got records for soliciting!'

'I understand, sir. But luckily they had mobile phones and recorded the two officers demanding sex acts and threatening them with arrest if they didn't comply.'

There was a long silence. Then, 'Bugger!'

'I'm sure it will stand up in court, sir.'

'Jones. It sounds suspiciously like entrapment. Did you instruct the two women to make a recording?'

'I couldn't possibly say, sir.'

'Jones, this is bloody stupid. One of the men was an MI5 agent. We won't be allowed to put him in court - it will break his cover. And if one can't be charged then the case collapses against DS Cooper. Just drop the charges, Jones. Let's try to smooth this over.'

Ken's face hardened. His superior should have known. He detested men who abused women and when it was law officers this was a gross betrayal of public trust. 'I don't think I can do that, sir.'

'Bloody hell, Jones. This won't help your career! I won't accept that answer. Think it over man. Get back to me on it!' And the phone was slammed down at the other end.

Ken turned to Jenny. She had overheard much of what was said. 'You're doing right, boss. What will you do if they drop the charges?'

'Kick up a stink. We'd better ring Tracey and get her to email the recording to us.'

'You think HQ'll try to delete it?'

'I hope not. But without it, we've no case. I'd like to be sure.'

'I'll call her now, boss.'

He realised he had to go over the head of his line manager. He sent a text message to the Deputy Chief Constable who was the national police coordinator for violence against women and girls. He'd heard her talk about the way that public confidence in the police had been shaken by cases of abuse of women by officers and he knew that she took it very seriously indeed. If anyone insisted on pulling rank on him over this, he'd look to her for back up and make initial contact immediately.

And it was as he completed the text that a very distressed Annette came rushing into the incident room like a rudderless ship in a storm. Her eyes darted round, looking for the best person to approach with her news. Someone who might perhaps be less critical of what Emma had done. She showed visible relief when she saw Jenny and gestured to her anxiously, wanting her to come to the entrance hall so they could talk without others hearing.

'You okay Annette?'

She began to gabble, so distressed at the news she had to give. 'It was Emm! My daughter Emma! She took it from the pram!'

Jenny held her arm reassuringly, trying to calm her down. 'Have you found it? The baby?'

Annette nodded almost lost for words. Her heart was beating so fiercely in her chest that breathing was difficult. 'Yes it's…but it's…'

Jenny pulled away. 'Stay here! I need to let the DI know! Don't move! It'll be all right!'

Annette attempted to stop her, but Jenny was fit and strong. She broke away and ran to where her boss was still processing the conversation he'd just had on the phone. 'Boss! We may have it! Oh my God! We might have found it!'

Ken joined them immediately, his face betraying both hope and doubt. 'Where?'

Jenny twisted round to face Annette. 'At your place?'

'The garden – in the shed…but…'

'The car!' Ken didn't wait for more details. The sooner they got to the baby the better. He held the rear door open for Annette and then jumped in beside Jenny. She drove as Annette tried to form sentences, but Ken shushed her. 'Don't worry. Let's just see what state she's in.'

There was no other traffic on the quiet narrow roads, and they arrived at Annette's in seconds.

She stumbled out of the car and looked helplessly at the gate. 'They're in there...Emma and her friends...waiting for us. I told them to wait. I came as soon as I knew. They're in the back...the garden...by the shed...they use it as a den...'

Ken again tried to calm her and then pushed open the gate, holding it for Jenny. Annette tried one last time to break the news she was desperate to tell. 'It's been there all this time! But it's...'

But the two detectives were out of sight and Annette stumbled after them, trying to tell them more before they met up with Emma.

Ken and Jenny halted at the door to the shed. Through the small, grimy window, three tiny faces peered out at them, guilty and afraid. Jenny stepped forward, making soothing sounds. 'Hello there. Don't be scared. We just need to see the baby. We need to check she's all right. Have you been looking after her all this time? It's been fun, has it? You've been proper little mothers, haven't you?'

Three pairs of eyes gazed back from the gloom. Three heads puzzled over the ways of grown ups. Why were they all so excited? What had they done that was causing so much fuss? They knew they shouldn't have taken her, but really – this was too much.

Jenny reached down and gingerly picked up the bundle of sheets and blankets that they had wrapped around little Summer to keep her warm.

She gently moved a cloth – one of the children had lent her own comfort blanket - and uncovered the child's face. She stared at it for what seemed an eternity then passed it, wordlessly to Ken.

'Is this what you took from the pram?' They nodded, dumbly. 'The pram outside Margot's house?' More nods. Where the lady lives who's lost her baby?' Nods again. 'You saw this in the pram and you took her?'

Emma, wide eyed, decided to defend herself. 'We'd have given her back. I wouldn't have kept her. But there was so much fuss I was scared. I didn't think grown ups…'

Jenny bent down, her face level with Emma's. 'No. I didn't either. They don't normally, do they? But to Margot this was very, very special. Just like you have dolls and pretend they're real babies. It was her baby, you see.'

Emma didn't, but nodded in agreement to humour her. Annette had caught up with them. 'I'm so sorry! I tried to tell you!'

Jenny handed the bundle to Ken. He gazed at it in astonishment, then focused his thoughts. 'Sorry Annette, it was our fault. We rushed things a bit. Well, this explains a lot.'

Jenny nodded. 'Why there was no-one seen on CCTV around Margot's house, except children. Why traces of DNA similar to Annette's were found on the cot.'

Ken nodded. 'And why Margot took her life. It wasn't just the shame of her gender identity being discovered. It was her neighbours finding out that they'd been searching for...this.'

The three adults stared at the bundle in Ken's arms. He had pulled the sheet away from her face. The doll stared back at them, with wide unseeing eyes.

Silence. And then Ken continued. 'She didn't just want to identify as a woman. She wanted a baby to make it complete. And so she invented one. And loved it and cared for it just like a real child.'

Annette began to cry. 'It's so sad!'

Jenny was more practical. 'It explains how uncommunicative she was when we first arrived. She never spoke, did she?' Annette shook her head. 'She must have been devastated that the baby was lost, but terrified that it would be found, and her secret would come out!' (Much later, a forensic psychiatrist explained that Margot was suffering from Narcissistic Mortification - so ashamed of what she had done and so afraid of it being revealed that she chose to take her own life rather than face up to the consequences.) There was still the possibility of doubt. Jenny continued: 'But we need to be sure that this is it. Annette, you stay with the children to make sure they're not too distressed. Boss, let's go back to Margot's house. I know how we can check it out!'

Ken didn't argue. Within seconds they were

pulling up outside Margot's. Jenny pushed past the policeman at the gate and went round the narrow path to the rear. The dustbins were untouched, She opened the rubbish bin and pulled out two of the orange plastic bags, supplied to safely dispose of soiled, disposable nappies. Jenny held them out so that Ken could see them. 'If these are dirty, there really was a baby and we need to keep looking. But if not...'

She pulled open the first one and, gingerly, emptied out the contents. It was an unused nappy, as clean as it had been when it left the factory. She smiled and dropped it back into the bin. The second orange bag was opened. The same. Margot had been playacting, had changed the baby as if it was a real child, but the nappies were spotless.

Jenny held the second one out to show Ken. 'Looks like the search is over, boss!'

Ken busied himself writing up his report and closing down the incident room at the village hall. Jenny was with Annette and Emma, who was crying and still afraid that she'd be in terrible trouble. Between her mother and the nice lady detective, they squeezed the truth out of her. Emma struggled to explain why she had done it. She had gone to the pram to see the baby. She liked real babies and had never had a glimpse of Summer. When she moved the blanket, she saw not the baby but a doll. She'd picked it up to hug it, surprised to find one there. She knew grown ups didn't have dolls (at least no adult she knew) and it was far too big for a baby to play with. It must, to her mind, be there by mistake.

Emma wanted to show it to her friends. She was going to put it back. But after she placed it in a makeshift crib in her den and called on her classmates to come to see it, she realised the police had been called. She was quickly aware that a huge hunt had begun. Emma was terrified, thinking that they were all looking for the doll she'd 'borrowed' and too afraid to tell anyone that it was there, in the garden shed. She had no idea that the police were actually searching for a real child that never existed. In her innocence she believed that grown-ups knew what they were doing and didn't make mistakes.

DI Jones thanked the last of the team as they left the hall, carrying the remainder of their equipment, and the village volunteers who were stacking the chairs and tables and cleaning the floor. He had imposed a news blackout so the villagers speculated wildly but quietly as they went about their tasks. It was generally concluded that Summer had been found, but not alive. Ken was conscious of their chatter but did nothing to confirm or deny the rumours. When the outcome was finally made public, it needed to be handled sensitively. He would leave it to the Police PR unit but was wondering whether he could share the news in confidence with the crime reporter, Wendy Seymor. She had been both sensible and discreet before, after all. And meeting her again seemed to Ken a not undesirable idea.

But before he could contact her, as he stood in the now empty and echoing hall, a call came through from the Assistant Chief Constable. She was a fiercesome lady whose withering criticism had reduced experienced coppers to gibbering wrecks on many occasions. He'd crossed swords with her over the death of Alec Bartle last year not far from where he was now standing. He'd suspected her of trying to protect one of the suspects, a high-ranking member of the House of Lords.

'Jones?'

'Ma'am.'

'I understand you've completed the missing baby case.'

'It turns out, ma'am, that the child was in fact a doll that the mother was treating as a real child. A very tragic case, ma'am. It had been picked up by a child who had no idea that a major investigation was being carried out.'

The response was icy. 'An investigation that has taken hundreds of man hours and cost many thousands of pounds. We'll be seeking retribution, suing the mother for the costs incurred by this needless waste of police resources!'

'Yes, ma'am. Tragically the lady in question is dead. She committed suicide yesterday.'

'Why have I not been informed? I should have been kept up to date on this, Jones!'

'A full report has just been finished, ma'am. It's on its way to you now.'

'I see. On a major incident like this, Jones, you should be sending daily reports. See to it in future!'

'Ma'am.'

'This Christian Retreat murder has just blown up in our faces again. You'll know that Anti-terror took it over. Scotland Yard has passed it back. Damn annoying. It appears that none of the traces sent to them matches any known terrorist. It's back in our hands. You started work on this, didn't you?'

'Yes, ma'am.'

'It'll save time if you pick it up again now your current case is over. But Jones. This arrest you made. It'll have to be cancelled. Grow up, man. I'm not going to argue with you on the rights of sex workers, but we can't treat senior officers this way. And putting a guard on them at the hospital! Really! They're hardly likely to run for it, are they!'

'Ma'am…'

'It was a rhetorical question, Jones. It doesn't require a response. You're a promising officer. But it's time to grow up. If police work were simply a case of right and wrong, life would be a lot simpler. But it's not. I don't want to hear any more about it. Get to – where is this damn retreat? – Marnhull, and do your job, man!'

'Yes, ma'am. But I want to put on record that I'm not happy about this, ma'am.'

'You'll be a bloody lot more unhappy if you don't let it drop.'

And the call was cut off. Ken, disconsolate, picked up the last of his papers and walked to his car to join Jenny. He was determined that Baxter and Cooper would pay for what they did. He decided to follow up the text he'd sent to the senior officer who'd been placed in national charge of offences against women by serving officers. He would talk to her. It would set his career back, he knew, but he couldn't live with himself if they just got away with what they'd done.

It was a twenty minute drive to Marnhull, via Hinton St. Mary. It gave him time to fill Jenny in on what had happened. 'Let me get in touch for you, boss. I've got less to lose.' Ken was touched by her offer, but no – this was something he had to see through himself.

They turned in at the gate. Ken felt a steely determination. He was certain that Drake, the self-styled prophet, was a con man taking advantage of a group of gullible women both sexually and financially. It was time to bring him down.

Drake was standing at the door as they approached. They were met with a look of genuine surprise. 'I wasn't expecting to see you again! The officers told us they were leaving and there was no reason for us to fear any further intrusion.'

Ken stepped closer to him than was comfortable, towering over him. 'I'm sorry to hear that. You've been misinformed!'

'Why? What's happened?'

'Well, sir, some further information has come to light that means we need to ask you and your 'flock' additional questions.'

Drake looked suddenly shifty. 'Oh? What information?'

'Perhaps we could come inside, sir.' He didn't wait for a response. Ken pushed past Drake into the entrance hall, closely followed by Jenny. 'We're looking at recent activity between the women here and their solicitors. A number of them have drawn up new wills.'

Drake's eyes gave away the rush of panic that ran through him. 'Yes. I tried to deter them of course but they were so insistent. So kind. They wanted to ensure that the work goes on you see. The Lord's work. With these donations, we can spread the word further...'

'Have you borrowed money on the promise of these future bequests?'

Drake looked as if he would rather be anywhere but there. The apocalypse couldn't come soon enough. 'Possibly. A little. To kick start the work...'

'And the recent death.'

'Tragic. A most valued member of our congregation!'

'Valuable. Because just before she was killed, she wrote a will leaving everything to you!'

'She did? I knew nothing, of course!' His face was ashen.

'We've only your word for that, sir. In the meantime, in the light of this new information and the recent hospitalisation of one of the sisters, we need to question them all again.'

'All of them? Surely not...'

'And you need to know that members of my team have been going through all your bank details for the past three months, and those of everyone else at the retreat. I am sure your conscience is clear, sir. So, you've nothing to fear from that, have you?'

It was obvious that Drake was much less confident than Ken pretended to be. He was shaking visibly. 'So if you'll arrange for everyone to come to the meeting room, my sergeant will interview them one by one.' Eager to get away, Drake turned and scurried towards the stairs. 'Sergeant Grace will go with you, sir. I'm sure you wouldn't try to prompt them as to what to say, but, well, just in case, eh?'

Drake was by now so unsteady on his feet that he stumbled over the first step. This gave Ken time to whisper, 'Just concentrate on the ones who you think might crack, Jenny. I'll go after the dead woman's husband. I don't suppose that Baxter or Cooper even bothered to interview him and no-one from our team was allowed to.'

They had the address from Sister Charity's driving licence. She had lived in Winterborne Kingston, about twenty miles away. It would take over half an hour on Dorset's winding roads, but Ken was grateful for the break. It gave him time to calm down and get his thoughts in order. He knew the top brass were going to be extremely angry with him when he went over their heads on the Cooper and Baxter arrests. It would set his career back. This might be the last case he would lead for a while. He wanted to end it well. He was certain that Drake had something to hide. It would have been in his interest to kill Sister Charity. Not only would he gain financially, but he would also avoid an embarrassing pregnancy that could have led to a very public divorce and the end of his masquerade as a man of God.

He just hoped that the sister's ex-husband was at home. It was moving towards early evening. More and more office workers seemed to leave for home around four o'clock. There was a chance.

He drove past The Greyhound Hotel to a new estate just beyond. Yes, these houses must have cost at least half a million. He turned off the main road and followed the numbers until he came to a smart three bedroomed detached. There was a car in the drive. He knocked and the door was opened by a youngish man with thinning hair. He was still wearing a suit but he'd loosened his tie and kicked off his shoes. This made him considerably shorter than Ken. He squinted up at him. Ken realised that he must normally wear spectacles but had put them down somewhere. He had a thin mouth and watery grey eyes. Ken thought it possible that Drake had seemed more attractive (he certainly had more charisma) than this man to Sister Charity and this might have led her astray.

'Mr Metcalf?'

'Yes?'

'Police. I'm Detective Inspector Jones of Dorset CID. I'd just like to ask you some questions about your late wife, Jean. May I come in?'

Metcalf didn't reply but moved aside slightly. Ken took this as an invitation to enter. The hall was covered with a thick pile shag carpet in a pale beige. Ken stood by the stairs and Metcalf led him, reluctantly, into the lounge. It had once had a woman's touch. The furniture was comfortable and modern. Fairly expensive sofas and an oak television stand and sideboard. The curtains were pretty and tasteful. But it looked as if it was sometime since it had been cleaned. And there were at least a dozen empty lager cans on the coffee table along with used crisp packets.

'Shall we sit down?' Ken asked, politely. Metcalf nodded and lowered himself into one of the sofas, but perched on the edge of it, looking anxious and uncomfortable. Ken felt something was wrong. The man wasn't acting like someone who had just lost his wife. The room looked as if it hadn't been cleaned for months. There was a rancid smell of fried food and grease. A thick film of dust covered all the polished surfaces. Metcalf seemed nervous and edgy rather than heartbroken.

'What is it you want to know?' Ken's eyes narrowed. He'd expect the man to want sympathy and any news about the investigation into his wife's death. But not this man. A strong suspicion began to form in his mind, and he completely changed his approach.

'We need to establish your movements on the day that the killing happened, just to remove you from any list of possible suspects.' Metcalf visibly paled and he edged even closer to the edge of the sofa. 'It's nothing to worry about. Just a formality. Can you tell me where you were on that evening between six pm and midnight?'

'Home. Watching the telly. I stayed in. I've never even been to Marnhull. Never.'

'I'm sure not, sir. Is there anyone who can verify your story?'

'Of course bloody not. The missus'd been away for months, living with that con artist pretending to be some sort of man of God...'

Ken decided to push him further. 'We found tyre tracks by the boundary fence to the retreat. Just to eliminate your car from our enquiries, I'll need to take screen shots of your car tyres. You've nothing to be afraid of, naturally, as you say you've never visited Marnhull.'

The look of panic on Metcalf's face was now unmistakeable. He blustered, 'But they're just tyres – I mean many cars, thousands, will have the same make of tyres...'

'Don't worry, sir. Modern forensics is very sophisticated!' He pretended that he was reassuring the man. 'Even if the suspect car has the same make of tyres as yours, there will be thousands of individual nicks and scratches that will confirm that yours isn't the one we're after. To an experienced forensic scientist,' he said this particularly pointedly, 'a tyre track is as individual as a fingerprint. Men have been convicted of the most grievous crimes,' this was stretching the point rather a long way, 'on no more evidence than this!'

All the time Ken was watching Metcalf's face. By now he knew that this man had a great deal to hide. If he'd stayed on the case, he told himself, he'd have called on the deceased husband later that same day, when he was first alerted to the body at the retreat. But those two clowns had taken over, convinced it was terror related and for the next few days he'd been on a wild goose chase for a baby that didn't exist. He was increasingly sure that he was in the same room as Jean Metcalf's killer. He decided to just push him a few inches further.

'We'll also need samples of your DNA and a piece of your hair. Some hairs from the killer were found on your wife's body. And some of his DNA was plastered onto her head, where she'd been pulled backwards before he knifed her. Of course, you've nothing to be anxious about. Because you were never there. It's just a formality. It's just to eliminate you from our enquiries!'

Oddly, Metcalf looked as if he had a great deal to be anxious about. He was sweating profusely now and one of his legs was visibly twitching. He put a hand on his knee to try to control it, but to no avail. It simply drew further attention to his state of panic. 'If you wouldn't mind waiting here a minute, sir, 'Ken said, gently, 'I'll be back in a moment. I just need the swabs from the car.' He looked round. If the man tried to escape, he could use a route through the kitchen. From what he could see of the rear garden there was a fairly high fence. It wouldn't be easy to climb. And with Ken at the car, he had no chance of escaping via the front. He smiled reassuringly as he left the house. As soon as he was on the drive, he called base. He'd need back-up to make an arrest. He took swabs from the glove compartment and, turning to make sure he wasn't seen, he also took a set of handcuffs and pocketed them.

When he re-entered the lounge, it was empty. The patio doors were open. He strode up to them. Metcalf was struggling to leap over the garden fence, to escape into a neighbour's garden at the rear. The fence was six feet high. Even in his desperation this was hard work for Metcalf. He had both hands on the top and was trying to pull himself over. His feet swung this way and that searching for a foothold. Ken was certain that he would fail. He watched calmly. The more he struggled, the more he proclaimed his guilt. Then one foot struck a nail that had held a length of trellis, long gone. It gave him the leverage he needed. Using this as a fulcrum, he swung the other leg over and then toppled inelegantly out of the garden.

Cursing under his breath, Ken gave chase. Taller and stronger than Metcalf, he was able to jump at the fence, get his arms over the top and haul himself up so that he could see over. The evenings spent in the police gym, working out, were paying dividends. He watched as Metcalf, stumbling as he ran, crashed into a recycling bin and sprawled across his neighbour's drive, before cursing and scrambling to his feet. Ken rolled over the top of the wooden fence and landed like a gymnast on the lawn below. He needed to get to the front of the house in time to see where his suspect ran next.

As he emerged into the front garden, he saw Metcalf run between two parked cars and dip down an alley that bisected two homes opposite and provided a pathway into a patch of woodland. Ken raced after him, enjoying the chase. He was confident of catching him. He was gaining with every stride. As he ran, Ken became more and more angry. If this man had killed his wife – and flight seemed to confirm his guilt – it was a terrible crime. Yes, she had been unfaithful and preferred another man to him – but that was no reason to murder her and her unborn child. In Ken's mind, he was in pursuit of a callous killer and he felt no qualms. If he had to use violence to bring him to heel, so be it.

Ahead of him, Metcalf dodged between two trees, but then stumbled over a root and fell. Ken grabbed one of the man's ankles. He expected him to attempt to pull free, but instead Metcalf kicked out with his other foot, catching Ken on the side of the head. Ken tried to catch the flailing leg so that he couldn't repeat the kick, but desperation provided the man with far more strength than he'd normally possess. He was kicking now with both feet – wildly – but some blows were landing home. Ken let go and looked down at the sprawling man as he wriggled and writhed, trying to get to his feet.

Ken realised that grabbing feet was going to be ineffective, so he aimed a kick at the man's solar plexus. It landed with a sickening thud. This was a good place to strike for two reasons. First, it would make it difficult for him to breathe and therefore render him helpless. Second, it left little visible mark in case of any subsequent complaint.

Metcalf lay for a few seconds, fighting for breath. Although largely incapacitated, he made one last attempt at freedom. He staggered to his feet and aimed a weak and wild blow at Ken's head. The detective watched it coming with a look of contempt, dodged at the last second, caught the man's wrist and twisted hard. Metcalf gave a scream of agony as he turned over in the air and crashed to the ground with a satisfying thud. Ken could sense a bruise forming on his cheek from one of the kicks that Metcalf had aimed at him. He grinned with satisfaction as he pulled one of Metcalf's arms high up his back, twisting it just enough so that it delivered the maximum pain without actually breaking.

It worked. Metcalf screamed and sobbed, begging him to stop. Ken didn't release his grip until he had him securely handcuffed. His captive wailed, as if determined to justify everything he had done even before he was charged with any offence. 'What would you have done, eh? Bloody hell, man – would you have left them at it? Let me bleeding go! I just did what any bugger would have done!'

Ken hissed in his ear, 'You don't have to say anything, you scum bag, but anything you do say...'

Metcalf didn't let him finish. 'Three years we'd been trying for a kid! She was everything to me – every bloody thing! Then she runs off with this bearded effing con artist and she texts me! Bloody texts me! She wants a divorce! She's pregnant! She's only been bloody shagging him and he's got her banged up! I'm going to marry him, she says and have his kid!'

Ken continued to hold him down. 'So what did you do?'

'I went there! To reason with her! To bloody beg her to come back! I'd even have let her keep the bastard! I got through the fence and then I saw them! Naked! Stark naked all of'em! And Jean – I found her, lying in the grass with that weirdo! So I went back to the car and got a blade from the toolbox. Went back to the clearing and he'd gone! Probably off to screw another of those bleeding stupid women! And there she was, with her back to me! With her arms up in the air! Praising God for all he'd bloody done for her! What would you have done, eh? If you were half a man – you'd have done the same as me! I went up behind her and pressed the knife against her neck! I wasn't going to cut her! I wanted her to listen! To stop and hear sense! But the stupid bint panicked – fell forward – the knife went in her neck! I couldn't help it!

There was blood spurting every bloody where! I just panicked! I ran off! I didn't even know she was dead!'

Ken put his hand over the man's mouth and stared him in the eye. 'You didn't ask for help. You didn't call an ambulance! You just left her there to bleed to death.' Metcalf burst into uncontrollable sobs. 'You'll be able to tell your story to a judge. A jury might take pity on you! But for now, you're under arrest for the murder of your wife Jean Metcalf!'

He pulled him to his feet. The fight had all left him. He allowed himself to be helped back to the front of his house, where a police car was parked, its blue lights flashing, the two officers staring at the front door wondering where Ken had gone. Several neighbours were at their doors watching as Metcalf was bent down and helped into the back of the car. Ken shut the front door of the house and then sat in his own car, with his head in his hands for a moment, thinking of the tragedy that had taken place: lives ruined, a neat suburban detached now to be known for all time as the home of a murderer. And the motive was jealousy.

He remembered Sheila. She'd made him jealous enough: when the woman he thought he loved was sleeping with her boss and asked him to hold off until she could sort things out. But would he have killed for it? Of course not. But it wasn't the same thing, was it? He wasn't married to her. She wasn't carrying someone else's child. Couldn't of course, he thought drily. His rival was old and had been snipped. No chance of pregnancy. But if his situation had been closer to that faced by Metcalf? He couldn't know. He hoped he wouldn't have been driven to violence, but he was honest enough to admit that he could be. There were some things, and not just crimes, that brought out a dark side in him. Even in this arrest, he knew that he'd used more force than he needed to and – this was the worst – he'd almost enjoyed it.

Sheila. There was still a message on his phone. He hadn't responded yet. She wanted to see him tonight. He had slept with her two nights ago, even though he knew it was wrong. She had offered herself to him, true. But he should have turned her down. Accepting the offer had just led to unreal expectations. It had complicated his life and his relationship with her. If he wasn't absolutely certain about his feelings for her, he should have walked away, no matter how tempting she was.

And there was a message from Jenny. She had taken Drake in for questioning. A number of women had made complaints about him when she had got them on their own. He had unfinished business there too. It was time to tidy up any misunderstandings between him and her – to clear the air.

The final message was from Wendy Seymor. Another offer to meet. He chewed for a moment on his bottom lip. It could be useful. He didn't know what PR had decided to release about the conclusion of the lost baby case. But Wendy seemed level-headed enough to discuss it sensibly. He judged that together they could come up with some ideas on how to handle it without causing unnecessary embarrassment for the good folk of Bishop Farthing, who'd been so duped by Margot. It wouldn't do any harm to meet up. And it would be a business meeting, of course. Of sorts. And so he'd have an excuse to put Sheila off at least another night. He texted Wendy. 'Where? What time?'

'The Botany Bay, About 8pm?'

'It's a date!' Ken considered this. Then deleted it and put, 'See you there.'

One Month Later

As Ken walked through the corridors of HQ towards the office of the Assistant Chief Constable, he went through the outcomes of the case in his head, knowing that he'd be called to account.

He'd left Jenny to deal with the angry women at the retreat. Not angry at her, but at Drake. The bishopric had decided that he was no longer a welcome tenant. After all that had happened, he'd been told to vacate the building within a week. He was unable to find alternative premises so soon, so had to announce to his acolytes that the group would be disbanded until a new home could be secured.

Unfortunately for him, several of them had already concluded that he was a false prophet. Jenny's questioning, her probing on his financial exploitation of them, her questioning of his morals and the attack by Sister Luke instigated by the sexual jealousy he had perpetrated amongst them had been enough to open their eyes. Drake was now under arrest, charged with multiple counts of fraud and sexual assault.

As for Metcalf, he was in prison awaiting a trial that would be a formality. He had made a full confession. The two cases linked together well. He was confident that justice would be served.

His worry centred on the cases of gross abuse of public office he had brought against Baxter, Cooper and the traffic officer who had photographed the naked body of Metcalf's wife. He had deliberately gone against orders. He suspected that this call to HQ was a reckoning. He tried not to think about the possible consequences. Getting worked up would do him no good. He needed to stay calm and rational, be able to explain clearly his reasons and wait for the judgement. He breathed slowly and steadily as he approached the ACC's office door and knocked.

No response at first. Seconds passed. He wondered if he should knock again. Then a faint noise. Was it someone inside calling 'Come in'? He couldn't be sure. Finally, he decided to take a chance. He had no choice. He turned the handle and pushed the door open. For a brief moment he had a fantasy vision – that he had misread the instruction and that, as he entered, he would see the ACC bent over her desk with the Chief Constable bonking her. It didn't happen, of course, but it meant that he entered the room with a slight smile on his face. Perhaps he ought to have looked more serious.

'Good morning, ma'am. You wanted to see me?'

She leaned back in her chair. Her lips were thin and severely set. Her cold eyes glared unblinkingly at him. She gave the impression that she was staring at something that had come out of the bottom of a dog. He wasn't invited to sit. He had to remain on his feet like a schoolboy who had misbehaved, facing the wrath of a headteacher. She pushed a newspaper towards him. He was able to catch the headline. 'Police called to account again for violence against women!'

'You've become quite a celebratory, haven't you, Jones?' The words were dripping with acid.

'Ma'am?'

'Maybe you haven't had a chance to read it?'

'No ma'am.'

She pulled the paper back and perched reading glasses on her nose before quoting from the page, with a sharp edge of sarcasm. 'The new star of Dorset CID, Detective Inspector Kenneth Jones, has become a whistle blower in defence of women everywhere by reporting three of his colleagues for gross misconduct in public office! Jones, 31, has created a stir since joining the Dorset force, not only for his good looks, but also for his effectiveness in bringing criminals to justice!' Ken squinted at the by-line: 'An exclusive from our chief crime reporter, Wendy Seymor.'

He sighed.

'Well?'

'Ma'am?'

'Remind me, Jones. Weren't you given explicit instructions that these charges should be dropped?'

'Ma'am.'

'Help me here, Jones. What part of drop these charges did you not understand?'

'I'm sorry, ma'am. It was a matter of principle.'

She looked at him pitifully, as if he was several pennies short of a shilling. She had another piece of paper in front of her. She picked it up and pretended to study it. 'I'm looking at your salary details, Jones. Whose paying you? Does it say Mr Principle?' She scanned it thoroughly. 'No, oddly not. It appears you're paid by Dorset Police Force. So who's giving you orders?' He didn't reply. He was sure he wasn't expected to. 'We are, Jones. And we're paying you. If you think you can live on what your principles will pay you, then resign!'

'In my defence, ma'am, these officers are a disgrace to the force. If we are to keep the confidence of the public, we must be prepared to expose and shame them – prove to women everywhere that this kind of despicable conduct is unacceptable in a modern force. Ma'am.' He stood to attention. He'd prepared that in advance and thought it went well. No-one could argue with that.

'It is up to us, Jones, to make these decisions, not you. These men would have been reprimanded, taken off active duties, dismissed if necessary. The public would have been kept safe and the reputation of the force would have been left intact. As it is, your actions have seriously eroded confidence. Our PR department is currently being deluged with calls from media all over the world wanting every sordid detail of what these men did. Do you really think that this builds public confidence? You need to realise, Jones, that you are out of your depth here. Officers well above your pay grade are far, far better placed to make decisions on matters such as this than you.'

'Ma'am, I'm...'

'An embarrassment to the force, Jones. That's what you are. This pursuit of personal glory, of pandering to journalists, stops now. Understand? We have given serious thought to dismissing you or lowering your rank. There has, however, been some support from loyal colleagues who have spoken up in your defence. Under the circumstances, a letter of reprimand will be placed on your file. If this happens again, Jones, you won't be so lucky. Understand?'

'Yes, ma'am.'

'Those officers involved, charged with gross misconduct, will now lose their jobs and their pensions. I hope you're satisfied.' She didn't wait for a response. 'In the meantime, you'd better make yourself useful.' She passed him a file. 'A homeowner in Okeford Stourpaine was digging in his garden this morning to make the foundation for a fence post when he struck the body of a child. Get out there and investigate!'

Ken grasped the file, glad to get his teeth into another investigation. 'Yes, ma'am. Thank you, ma'am!'

'Dismissed, Jones!' As he turned smartly and walked into the corridor, the ACC smiled to herself. 'Let's see how quickly you can solve this, Jones! We estimate the body's been in the ground at least three hundred years!'

◆ ◆ ◆

Find out how DI Jones tackles this new murder mystery in the next book in this series: Death or Dishonour, the Garden of Death!

BOOKS BY THIS AUTHOR

Bishop Farthing

The story of how an isolated Dorset village survived the pandemic (just!) An account of how two fifty somethings find romance despite the restrictions of lockdown, and the hilarious ups and downs of their love story. It invites us to remember all the trials and tribulations of that time but with a humorous slant - encouraging us to recall - and sometimes laugh - at what was for many a worrying - even tragic - period in our lives, but one which we survived.

Don't Go Down To The Woods Today!

A DI Jones mystery: a body is found in the bluebell wood at Bishop Farthing and Ken Jones and his assistant Jenny Grace are led on an exciting chase that involves organised crime, sex trafficking and drug cartels! The story reaches a thrilling and unexpected conclusion! A must for anyone who enjoys an exciting story sprinkled with mystery and humour!

Printed in Great Britain
by Amazon